# PARTNERSHIPS CAN KILL

## by *Connie Shelton*

**Intrigue Press**

ISBN 0-9643161-4-5
LCCN 96-80482


First printing 1997

For Brandon

May you learn the joy of work
and the satisfaction of a job well done.

The author wishes to acknowledge the invaluable assistance of the following: Dan Shelton, as ever, my inspiration and lifemate; Gretchen Lemons and Mary Cimarolli-Robottom for their assistance in proof reading; Bill Conley, Chief (retired), Angel Fire, NM Police Dept. and knowledgeable PI.

**Other books by Connie Shelton**

The Charlie Parker Mysteries:
*Deadly Gamble*
*Vacations Can Be Murder*

Audio Books:
*Deadly Gamble*
*Vacations Can Be Murder*
*Partnerships Can Kill*

Non Fiction:
*Publish Your Own Novel: Get Your Book into Print
and Into the Stores Now!*

# 1

The Albuquerque airport has an ambiance all its own. Wooden chairs with leather seats fill the waiting areas. They are stiff and uncomfortable as hell, but no one would consider changing them because they have that "Southwest chic." Accents of turquoise and terra cotta set this airport apart from the look-alike terminals in other cities. As a lifelong resident of this southwestern city, my memories are of my brothers and myself as kids sitting on a low adobe wall, watching planes take off and land on Sunday afternoons. Coming home again makes my throat feel a little tight.

Emotion aside, if I'd known what lay in store for me within the next few days, I would've probably stayed on the plane.

The 737 rolled to a slow stop. There was a distinct *chunk* as the jetway connected. Sleepy passengers moved slowly, gathering belongings. I unfastened my seat belt. The remnants of my last pain killer were wearing off, and my head began to throb.

It was after ten o'clock and only a handful of people waited. They stood in an eager clump. Eager to meet loved ones, or eager to be back home in bed, I couldn't say. My brother, Ron, waited for me. He wore a muted plaid shirt, scuffed brown roper boots, and his straw Stetson, which he favors because it hides the fact that his hair is thinning on top. His faded Levi's bore permanent creases across the front and a whitened wallet-sized square on the right rear pocket. I hadn't seen him in ten days, and it seemed that his gut was perhaps a little less obvious over the top of his silver belt buckle. Ron dieting?

"Hey, kiddo, how was Hawaii?" He reached out to take my carry-on bag.

"It was murder." I could hear the tiredness in my own voice. We trailed the straggling crowd toward the escalators.

"I'll bet. All that lounging on the beach, all those mai-tais. Rough life."

"I meant that literally. It was murder." I lifted my hair in back to give him a glimpse of the fourteen stitches at the base of my skull.

"Charlie, *what happened?*"

"I'll tell you about it later," I promised. This would take longer than a walk through the airport would allow. "What's new around here?" I asked.

Did I imagine it or did he actually blush?

"Ronnnn . . . ?"

"Well . . . " He *was* blushing.

"It's a woman, isn't it? Tell me, or I'll . . . I'll . . . I don't know." I moved slightly ahead of him, and turned around, walking backward so I could watch his face. Ron has a stubborn streak a mile long that won't allow him to let his little sister push him around. He would stall a while longer just to make it clear that telling me was his idea, not mine. I fell back in step with him and kept quiet.

"Her name is Vicky." His voice started out quietly, but I could hear the enthusiasm grow as he talked. "She's pretty and has such a bubbly personality. We have so much in common, although she is a little younger than me."

"*How* little?" Ron is thirty-six, divorced, father of three. Responsible, dependable, but a prize catch?

"We met at Denim and Diamonds," he continued, "and we really hit it off, right from the start."

Picked up a girl in a bar? Really, Ron, in this day and age, where is your caution? I didn't have to say it; he got the message from the look I flashed him.

"I know, I know."

We arrived at the baggage carousel just as its obnoxious horn started whonking. Two little kids scurried off the stainless steel edge where they had been balancing on tip-toe. The crowd was pushy, it was late, and my head throbbed. I let Ron watch the bags revolve around the giant silver lazy Susan. I took a seat to the side, on a slatted wooden bench that dug into my butt in strange and painful ways.

I had only one suitcase and luckily it was among the first to come off the line. Ron was gentleman enough to carry it for me toward the parking garage.

"I can't wait for you to meet Vicky," he said, as he started his Mustang convertible. "She's really vivacious and fun-loving. I think you two might have lots to talk about."

I made some polite noises, but truthfully, I was beat and in no mood to talk about Vicky. There was a time when I could travel for days, eat rich food, stay up three nights in a row, and still go to work the next morning. No more. I was ready to get home, settle in, and pop another of my pain killers.

"Did you check in with Gram?" I asked.

"I sure did. Called every day and stopped by twice," he assured me.

"How was Rusty?"

"Rambunctious as ever."

I'd left my sixty pound dog in the care of my ninety pound, eighty-six year old neighbor. I wondered which of them would be happier to see me by now. I only hoped Rusty hadn't shed too much hair, lifted his leg on her begonias, or otherwise made her life stressful during the last week.

Ron successfully guided us through the low ceilinged airport parking garage. We emerged to a clear night, which was probably full of stars, except that there were too many bright lights around the airport to see them. I let myself sink back against my seat, the cool desert night air streaming through my hair and easing my headache, while he joined the sparse flow of traffic on I-25. Fifteen minutes later, we pulled into my driveway.

I'm probably one of the few thirty-year-old people anywhere these days who still lives in her childhood home. They called it a ranch style house back then, white brick with a shallow pitched roof. The three bedrooms, two baths, spacious living room, and big airy kitchen are really more than Rusty and I need, but a modern little box in an upscale part of town wouldn't come with the fifty-foot sycamores in the back yard, or my mother's Peace roses, whose canes are now thick as small tree trunks.

The living room lamp glowed behind the front drapes, operated by a timer, just as I'd left it. Ron carried my bag inside for me.

"You gonna feel like coming in tomorrow?" he asked. He wanted to ask about the cause of my fourteen-stitch headache, but refrained.

"I'll be fine," I assured him. "Some food and a good night's sleep are what I need right now."

"Okay, see you there."

Right now, I wanted to see Rusty. Without bothering to carry my suitcase to the bedroom, I headed for the back door.

I'd no sooner switched on the back porch light than I saw the one next door come on. Elsa Higgins, Gram to me and my brothers, was obviously watching for me, probably anxious to get to bed. Leaving my back door standing open, I followed the well-worn path to the break in the hedge between our two properties. I had not quite made it to the edge of her porch, when the big red-brown energy machine bounded out. His thick tail whipped my legs and he rubbed against me, covering my hands with slobbery kisses.

He grinned at me with that special smile of his that people frequently take for a snarl. With most people, I just let them think that.

Elsa stood in her doorway, looking smaller and more frail than I remembered. She lives alone, cleans her own house, plants a garden every summer, and makes lap rugs for the "old people" at her church. She's feisty and opinionated, and I want to be just like her when I grow up. She's been next door to me all my life, and saved my ass more than once since I lost my parents in a plane crash my junior year in high school. I wasn't sure whether I detected a certain amount of relief in her expression as she watched Rusty and me reunite.

"How was the trip, Charlie?"

"Fine. I brought you something, but I'll have to unpack to find it." I walked a bit closer to her, staying just far enough back that I wouldn't have to get invited in. "How about coming over for breakfast in the morning? I'll tell you all about it then."

That seemed fine with her. She's not much of a night person, anyway. Rusty and I headed back through the hedge. I was starving, and would have loved a plate of Pedro's sour cream chicken enchiladas, but I couldn't summon up the energy to get in the Jeep and drive the six blocks just now. The long flight and my throbbing head had taken a lot out of me. The only milk in the fridge smelled ten days old, so I settled for a bowl of granola with yogurt on top instead. Rusty flopped out on the kitchen floor, his brief moment of joy at my arrival long over. For him, it was like I'd never been gone. They say dogs have no sense of time. It must be true — he acts the same way if I walk out to the mailbox.

I rechecked all the windows and doors, then dragged my suitcase down the hall to my bedroom. I'd save the real unpacking for morning. Right now, I only wanted a shower and some sleep. After emerging from the steamy bathroom, I took one of my prescription painkillers and climbed between the cool sheets. Rusty took up his usual post on the rug at the foot of my bed. I slept like a dead person until the light coming through my window got my attention about seven.

# 2

My head felt a hundred percent better, and in a sudden burst of perkiness, I made my bed, unpacked my suitcase, got dressed, and moved toward the kitchen to start the coffee. Elsa showed up about five minutes after I raised the kitchen window shade, our long-time signal to let each other know when we're up and at 'em. Bless her heart, she brought a half carton of milk and warm blueberry muffins.

"I knew you wouldn't have time to go to the store yet," she said.

The smell of the Kona coffee I'd brought from Hawaii filled the kitchen, making my knees weak. I poured a couple of mugs full and let the caffeine course through my veins while I watched butter melt into the blueberry muffin. I filled her in briefly on the vacation, skimming lightly around the part about my head injury. I didn't want her to think I'd put my life in danger as a result of my acquaintance with the handsome helicopter pilot I'd met there, although I had. Drake Langston was a unique sort of man, whose illuminating smile and tender love-making had gone straight to my heart. He'd left me at the airport (was it only eighteen hours ago?), with the promise that we'd see each other again. Well, we'd see. Life had taught me that such promises are easily made, and rarely kept.

By eight-thirty, Elsa had come and gone. I figured I was as ready as ever to get to the office. I retrieved my briefcase from the front bedroom I now use as a home office. It was the boy's room when we were kids, but now I have my desk, computer, and a file cabinet with a few personal files in it. Rusty waited by the front door, beating his thick tail against the doorjamb.

"Okay, buddy, let's go." He nearly went into a frenzy before I could get the screen door open. He raced for the Jeep, wanting to ride up front in the passenger seat. I made him go to the back.

In ten minutes we covered the mile to our office, which occupies an old Victorian house just off Central Avenue. Huge trees, leafed out in pale spring green, formed a canopy over our quiet side street in this partly residential neighborhood. Lilac and snowball bushes flanked several doorways, filling the air with their sweet perfume. The yard service had apparently visited our gray and white gingerbreaded place in recent days. The lawn was freshly mown and the shrubs trimmed. I pulled into the narrow concrete drive that follows the left edge of the property to an old carriage house in the back yard. The Jeep edged into its regular spot between Ron's red convertible and Sally's imported four-by-four. The tiny flowerbed beside the back door sported freshly planted pansies. I smiled at their little purple faces.

Inside, we had converted the old living room to a reception area. The dining room has a big work table, although I'd still like to get something nicer, for conferences. The upstairs bedrooms are now Ron's and my offices.

Ron was already at his desk when I arrived, deeply engaged in a phone conversation which sounded as if it might be intensely personal. I bet myself that I'd get another earful about Vicky later on. I twiddled my fingers in his direction, and headed for my own office.

My antique desk looked about like I expected. I had left it spotlessly clean eleven days ago. Now a small mountain of unopened mail sat heaped in the center. The fresh flowers on the bookcase had been reduced to a vaseful of crispy stalks standing in slimy green water. I raised two sections of the bay window to give my hanging plants some spring air and carried the dirty vase to the bathroom. Rusty stretched out on a corner of the oriental rug, knowing we were in for the long haul.

Twenty minutes later I had the mail divided into three piles — Do Now, Do Later, and Circular File. I was just about to tackle the Do Now pile, which consisted of bills to pay, and phone calls to return, when I glanced up to find Sally Bertrand standing in my doorway.

Sally is our part-time receptionist. She's a big girl, what some might call "large boned," with small breasts and heavy thighs. She wears her wheat-colored hair in a shaggy style that looks like she whacks at it herself whenever the mood strikes, without benefit of a mirror for guidance. Her wide face has an honest sprinkling of freckles, and her ready smile shows teeth that are even, if not perfect. She's married to a bearded mountain-man of a guy, and their joint pleasure in life is hiking off to the most remote area they can find, while carrying a bare minimum of equipment. This is directly contrary to my way of thinking, where roughing it consists of black and white TV in a motor home.

Sally's overriding concern these past few months has been her effort to get pregnant. She's recently turned thirty, like me, and thinks she hears her biological clock ticking.

"What a mess, huh?" She nodded toward my desk.

"Yeah, but I suppose I'll get through it. How'd it go while I was gone?"

"Ron made me stay till five every day. He's really allergic to answering his own phone, isn't he?" She chuckled in her infectious way. "Have you met Vicky yet?"

"Not yet, but I suspect I'll soon have the pleasure. What's she like?"

Anyone else might be afraid to speak candidly about her boss's personal life, but I knew Sally would be honest with me. We have an informal, friendly relationship, despite the fact that I sign her paycheck.

"Young," she answered.

"How young? I noticed Ron neatly ducked the question when I asked him last night."

She rolled her eyes briefly upward. "Well . . . young enough to be his, um, much younger sister."

Oh, boy. I could hardly wait.

"By the way," she continued, "I'm a week late." She patted her tummy.

I made some weak-sounding congratulatory noises. I don't know — my biological clock must be in a different time zone than everyone else's.

"Well, I guess I better get back to Ron's letter to the state insurance commission," Sally said.

She left, obviating the necessity for me to comment further on her possible state of motherhood. I turned contentedly back to paying bills. Call it accountant eccentricity.

By eleven-thirty, I had all the accounts payable entered into the computer and was just about ready to start printing the checks. For some reason, I was having a heck of a time getting the forms to line up in the printer. I could feel my frustration level climbing at a rate corresponding to the hunger pangs in my stomach. I decided to tackle the problem again after lunch. I grabbed my purse and was about to switch off the lights, when I heard voices out in the hall.

"Charlie! You going out?" Ron stood just outside my doorway.

"Just to get some lunch. Want to join me?"

"I'd like you to meet Vicky," he said. He was beaming like a cat who'd just discovered a whole cage full of canaries. He stepped aside, his hand guiding Vicky toward me. Rusty roused around and headed toward her. Apparently not a dog person, she began to back up at the sight of him. I told him to sit in the corner and mind his own business.

Vicky and I shook hands graciously but there was no question that we were sizing each other up. My expectations hadn't been too far off the mark. She had to be in her early twenties. She wore a clingy jersey dress, in an electric shade of purple, which hit her a good six inches above the knees. Large purple hoop earrings, black hose with tiny black bows at the ankle, and black four inch heels completed her attire. Her dark hair was loose and fluffy, caught up on one side by a comb of some kind. Her face still had a lot of the fullness they used to call baby fat, although there's probably a more sensual sounding name for it now. Her makeup was impeccably done, and I imagined her working at the Estee Lauder counter at The Broadway. She had a beauty mark at the left corner of her mouth, and I suppressed the desire to lick my finger and rub at it to see if it would come off.

"Well. I'll repeat the invitation. Would you both like to join me for lunch?" I hoped I sounded sincere.

"Thanks, Charlie," Ron said. "But we already had some other plans."

Vicky beamed at him and I got a pretty good idea what he meant, but thinking about it made my stomach feel kind of squeamish. I tried not to let my thoughts appear on my face

*11*

as I pulled my door shut and walked alongside Vicky down the stairs, then toward the reception area. Sally and I exchanged a look, and I told her I'd be back in an hour or so. I traveled toward the back, leaving the two of them standing by the front door.

The Jeep started with a little more roar than I'd intended, and I lowered the windows on both sides to dispel the stuffy air inside. As I came out the driveway I noticed Vicky's car, a red Firebird, parked at the curb.

I pulled out onto Central, going nowhere in particular. I wasn't really in the mood for fast food, but couldn't decide what, exactly, I was in the mood for. Five or six blocks later a burgundy colored awning caught my eye. I'd noticed the place several months ago, but had never tried it. Nouvelle Mexicano. Sounded rather different.

I found a somewhat tight parking space three doors down, and hoped an hour's worth of meter time would be enough. The restaurant was next to an old movie theater that, not being one of the new eight-plexes, was now relegated to showing B movies and cult classics. On the other side was a discount clothing store that appeared to generate quite a bit of traffic.

A stucco front had been added to the restaurant's narrow bit of sidewalk frontage, along with curlicued wrought iron window grates that were meant to be decorative and functional at the same time. I pulled on the heavy wooden door inlaid with a stained glass parrot and stepped into a shady foyer.

A hostess, who could have been no more than nineteen, greeted me with a dimply smile. She had a sleek French braid that went halfway down her back. Picking up a menu, she led me to a small table. The interior of the place consisted of one main room, divided into several sections by chest-high dividers, topped with green plants. The lighting was done in such a way as to suggest skylights, although being on the ground floor of a three story building, I knew there were none. The effect was light and modern. The color scheme was pale turquoise and mauve. The menu read like a crash course in foodspeak, with many items "delicately seasoned," "lightly sauteed," and "with a hint of . . . " It was Mexican with a health-food perspective. I chose a salad that sounded interesting, a combination of greens, chicken (briefly sauteed and impeccably seasoned), and herb cheeses, all in a tortilla shell "lightly tanned" in 100% canola oil. My waiter brought my iced tea almost instantly, and I sipped at it while scoping out the rest of the room.

The place was only about a third full, although my watch told me it was twelve-fifteen. Being a Friday, I would have expected this to be prime time in a downtown restaurant. My salad arrived just then, and I had to admit, it was delicious. Despite the overuse of adjectives on the menu, the food was just plain good.

"Charlie Parker?"

I looked up to see a woman leaning over my table. "Sharon? My goodness, imagine running into you here."

"I own the place," she said, her eyes proudly sweeping the room. "How is your meal?"

I told her what I thought.

"What's it been, now? Ten years?"

"Try twelve. Graduation day," she said. "I didn't see you at the tenth reunion, and wondered whether you were still in Albuquerque."

Sharon Ortega had improved with age. Her face was slimmer than I remembered, her hair shorter and lighter than before. She wore it in a breezy chin-length style, with generous streaks of blond highlights through it. Her eyes were still dark brown, about the size of quarters, with the same thick natural lashes we had all envied. She wore a crisply tailored linen dress of pale turquoise, and a wide silver bracelet on her right wrist. We'd shared classes throughout high school, although we had not palled around much outside school hours.

"What are you doing these days, Charlie?"

"My brother, Ron, and I have a private investigation firm together."

Her eyes got even wider. "Really? You chase down bad guys and everything?"

"Well, Ron's the licensed PI. I'm the accountant. But, you know how it goes. I tend to get dragged into cases from time to time." I handed her one of my cards. She stared at it for a good ten seconds, as if memorizing the details.

"How about you?" I asked. "How long have you had the restaurant?"

"We've been open about a year," she answered. "I have a partner, too. I manage the kitchen and the help, and he handles the paperwork. Hey, you and he might just hit it off. You got anyone special in your life right now?"

I thought of Drake Langston. "No one permanent yet," I told her.

"I think David's around someplace." She glanced around the room.

"That's okay, don't interrupt anything." I really didn't want any hasty matchmaking on my behalf, so I quickly changed the subject. "How's business, Sharon? You like being downtown?"

She shifted from one foot to the other, and I could see a flicker of emotions cross her face, as she decided how much to tell me.

"It's been all right," she said cautiously. "We really started off with a bang a year ago. We're only open for breakfast and lunch, you know, and we had people lined up out the door. Lately, though, I don't know." Her voice dropped to little more than a whisper. "I guess maybe the fad's over."

"The food is great. I'd think the healthy approach would be really big now."

"That's what we thought, too. I took a lot of my mother's old recipes and adapted them. Cut out a lot of the frying, switched everything to unsaturated, lean, fresh. Everyone who tries us really seems to like the result.

"I don't know," she continued. "Maybe it's just this city."

I knew what she meant. I've seen it happen many times. A new restaurant will be a huge hit at first, then business falls off, and soon they're gone.

"Well. I better let you finish your lunch." She pulled her shoulders a little straighter and summoned a bright smile. "Enjoy."

I watched her make the rounds of the other tables, while I finished my salad. She had a few words and a friendly smile for each of her customers. She looked like the old Sharon I had known, outgoing and friendly with everyone.

The waiter had left my check, and I was calculating the tip when I felt someone approach. I glanced up to see Sharon once more, this time toting a man behind her.

"Charlie, this is my partner, David Ruiz," she said.

We exchanged hellos, and I made a couple of comments about how much I'd enjoyed my lunch. David seemed eager to be somewhere else. He was in his late twenties, well dressed in gray summer weight wool slacks and a custom made shirt with monogram on the pocket. His shoes were Gucci, and his dark hair looked like it had been trimmed within the past two days. Sharon had probably dragged him away from his desk. His shirt sleeves were rolled up, and I saw a smudge of blue ink on his right middle finger. He had a handsome face, but some difficulty in cracking a smile. As we talked, his eyes darted around distractedly. I stood up, giving him a chance to exit.

Later, I would wish I'd talked a little longer with David

Ruiz. The next time I would hear his name would be when I learned that he was dead.

# 3

Ron wasn't back yet when I arrived at the office. Sally said there hadn't been any calls. She had her desk cleared and her car keys out, apparently eager to leave for the day. I secretly hoped Ron wouldn't come back for awhile yet. There were no appointments on the book, and I could use the time alone to get my own work caught up.

I went back up to my own office, where Rusty greeted me like I'd been gone a week. I slipped him a biscuit from a canister I keep on my shelf. I spent the rest of the afternoon finishing up the payables, then getting on to some letters and phone calls. By four o'clock things were beginning to shape up. It would be another week before I'd have to worry about the month-end financials, so all in all I felt good about the amount of work I'd accomplished.

I still hadn't heard from Ron, so I left him a note telling him that I'd like to go over the pending cases with him. If he got in before seven and wanted to come by the house, I was making spaghetti. I figured that would lure him, if nothing else would. I called his apartment, and left a similar message on his answering machine.

Rusty trotted around after me, his toenails clicking on the hardwood floors, as I checked the front door lock, closed windows, switched off the copy machine and the lights. We ended up in the kitchen at the back of the old house, where I wiped off the counter tops, threw out the old coffee grounds, and washed out the pot. At four-thirty, we locked the back door and headed for the Jeep, parked behind the building. Rusty made a side trip to the back corner of the property, where he did his business, then feeling much relieved, he jumped into the back seat.

I made a quick stop at the grocery store to stock up on milk, bread, and salad ingredients. It was still only five-fifteen when I got home. Ron had left a message on my machine saying that he would love spaghetti for dinner, and would be there at six-thirty.

Ron had two cases currently going. One was a pretty standard matter of gathering evidence in a workman's comp case. The man who claimed a totally debilitating back injury had somehow managed to play two sets of tennis the previous Saturday, according to rumor. Ron's job now, was to get pictures, testimony, whatever it took to prove that the guy really should be back at work.

The other case involved a prominent businessman, Morris Boyd, who was apparently fooling around with the wife of a well-known politician. The businessman's wife, Lorraine Boyd, was our client. Since New Mexico has fairly lenient no-fault divorce laws, I could only guess that her reason for wanting the whole nasty little story in pictures was to facilitate some kind of blackmail, either monetary or emotional. I hate those kind of things, and I've told Ron I'd rather we didn't take them. But, with Ron, income is income. I've been fortunate enough with my investments that the agency is more of a side-line for me. Ron needs every penny he gets just to manage rent and child support.

We rehashed all of this over plates of pasta, salad, and garlic bread, all of which I must admit I threw together from packages and jars. Although I can cook when the need arises, I challenge myself to produce acceptable food in fifteen minutes or less, using nothing more than the microwave or toaster oven. We had stacked the dishes in the sink, and moved into the living room with glasses of red wine.

"You never did explain that little railroad track of stitches you have across the back of your skull," he reminded.

"Let's just say it turned out to be a working vacation," I told him.

"And how did you get talked into working on your vacation?"

This time, it was my turn to blush.

"A guy, huh?" he teased.

"Well . . . " I told him a little about Drake, and sketched an outline of the case, which had taken me from Kauai to San Francisco and back, and had given some revealing insights into the helicopter tour business in Hawaii.

"Look, Vicky and I are driving up to Angel Fire tomorrow morning for the weekend. Why don't you join us? It would give you a nice breather."

I could think of better ways to breathe than in the company of cute Vicky, but I didn't want to hurt his feelings by saying so. After all, I didn't know the girl, and to be fair, I should withhold judgement.

"I have a two bedroom condo reserved. It's two story, and you can have the lower floor all to yourself. You and Rusty."

I felt myself wavering. Angel Fire is one of the prettiest places in the entire state. Tucked into one corner of the wide green Moreno Valley, the little alpine village perches at the base of eleven thousand foot Agua Fria Peak, looking like something right out of a Swiss travel brochure. I'd been there a couple of other times with friends and loved it. During the winter months, it's a bustling ski resort, but in the summer the pace slows down considerably. The summer season kicks off Memorial Day weekend, another week away. Right now, it should be quiet and peaceful. I felt myself giving in to the idea. Ron could tell what I was thinking.

"Okay, then," he said, getting up to carry his glass to the kitchen. "We'll stop by and pick you up at eight."

"We better take my Jeep," I said. "I can't see three people and a dog jammed into that convertible of yours."

"You sure?"

"As long as you'll still do the driving."

He agreed, set his wine glass in the sink, and squeezed my shoulder as he left. I switched on the TV but couldn't get interested in anything. Dialed Drake Langston's number on Kauai. When the answering machine came on, I remembered the four-hour time difference and figured he wouldn't even be home from work yet. I left a brief message, saying that I was thinking about him, then wondered if I shouldn't be observing the old boy-girl ritual where girl waits for boy to call first. Too late now.

I puttered around the kitchen, washed the dishes, put the leftover salad in the fridge, and went around the house emptying waste baskets into a black plastic garbage bag. Tomorrow would be trash day. I carried my one sack out to the curb. That done and Rusty fed, I decided I was ready for a shower.

Twenty minutes later, I stood in front of my closet deciding on what clothes to take to Angel Fire. Mountain weather is always cooler, and sometimes more unsettled, than in the city. I tossed an extra pair of jeans, some boots, and two sweaters into a bag. The unfinished Clancy novel was in the living room.

I went to retrieve it and that's when I noticed the call on my answering machine. It must have rung while I was outside or in the shower.

"Hi, Charlie," Drake's deep voice came through. "Sorry I missed you . . . Been thinking about you constantly . . . uh, I guess I'll have to call back later. I have an association meeting to go to now. But then you'll probably be asleep . . . Well, I'll just try over the weekend. 'Bye."

A pang of longing shot through me. Maybe I should cancel the weekend plans with Ron and Vicky.

*Wait* a minute, I stopped myself. No way was I going to fall into that sitting-by-the-phone trap, that molding-my-life-to-fit-his routine. If anything were to develop between Drake Langston and me, it would have to come about naturally. And I *would not* lose sleep over making it happen. I tossed my packed duffle onto the floor, turned out the lights, and lay in bed with my eyes wide open until after one a.m.

# 4

The condo was situated near the base of the Angel Fire ski area. This time of year, ours was the only car in the parking lot. Rusty and I shared the downstairs bedroom. That and a small bathroom comprised the entire lower floor. The view from my window showed the side of the Jeep, not much more. I clipped a leash to Rusty's collar, and we left to explore. Ron and Vicky could unpack and get started with whatever else they had planned for the weekend. I didn't especially want to be around for that.

Outside, the sky was a deep blue. Tall ponderosa pines cast dappled shadows across the ground. A brisk wind came up the road, making the air at least fifteen degrees cooler here than in the city. I was glad I'd brought a light jacket along with the sweaters.

We walked uphill, toward the unmoving ski lift. No one else in sight. Rusty tugged constantly at the leash, so I finally gave up and unclipped it. He wouldn't go far, he just wanted the freedom to go at his own pace. He stayed with me, trotting within a few yards, wherever I walked.

Dried pine needles crunched under our feet. The air was crisp, free of the car exhaust and fast food smells associated with the city. I breathed deeply, absorbing all the oxygen I could, like a drug.

An hour later, puffing slightly from the altitude, we re-entered the condo. Vicky sat on the living room sofa, her eyes and hands intent on a video game connected to the TV set. She had changed from the stretch pants and halter top she had worn for the trip. Now she wore an oversize T-shirt and a pair of red socks. Her tan legs were bare. Ron was barefoot in the kitchen, putting food away in the refrigerator. Their bedroom door stood open, revealing rumpled bedding and clothing carelessly tossed on the floor. Suddenly I longed for Drake. I didn't want to make idle chit-chat with these two.

There was a small deck off the living room with several white plastic chairs on it. I picked up the Tom Clancy novel that I hadn't quite finished in Hawaii, and took it out to the deck. The deedle-deedle music from Vicky's video game disappeared when I closed the glass door.

I found myself thinking about Drake Langston more than I intended to. I wanted to tell myself that it had been a vacation fling, but I'm not given to flings, so that idea went against my grain.

By five o'clock the sun was low over the western hills, the tall pines casting cool shadows my way. I slid the glass door open. Video characters bounced across the TV screen. Ron dozed on the sofa, the sports section of the Albuquerque paper draped across his chest.

"I think I'll start some dinner," I suggested.

Neither of them replied. I walked between Vicky and the television without breaking her concentration. Rummaging through our provisions, I came up with a frozen lasagna, which I popped into the oven. Dumped pre-cut salad greens into a bowl. The condo came equipped with plenty of dishes and utensils, so I set the table and located a candle for the center. Ron roused at the sound of all the clinking and helped put the finishing touches on the salad. We whiled away the rest of the lasagna's baking time by taking turns challenging Vicky at the video game. My skills in this department are sadly lacking and I got eliminated early in the first round.

At last the lasagna bubbled and we pried the video game away from Vicky. Ron lit the candle on our table and held her hand as we took our seats.

"So, Vicky, Ron tells me you're a decorator," I said, once we'd scooped lasagna and salad onto our plates.

"Yeah," she answered, her dark eyes looking at Ron rather than me.

"Do you have a specialty? Residential or commercial?"

"Oh, just about anything."

"What's your preference in style? Traditional, contemporary?" I felt like I was giving her the third degree but she certainly wasn't volunteering anything.

She shrugged in answer to my question.

Ron piped up: "You should see Vicky's place, Charlie. She's really done a beautiful job with it."

"Great, I'd like that." I addressed the answer to Vicky, although she had not extended the invitation.

Ron sensed her reluctance to open up and he steered the subject to something else. After dinner, the two of them volunteered to do the dishes. Vicky laughed and talked with Ron, who had his arms in the soapy water. What was going on here? I could only guess that she just plain didn't like me.

I excused myself and took my dog and my Clancy novel downstairs to my room, where I could convince myself that being alone was just fine with me.

Sunday morning I awoke early, dressed and took Rusty out for a walk. We bought fresh muffins at the small market on the highway and listened to the bells at the white steepled church chime out hymns half-remembered from childhood. I shared my muffin with Rusty. Despite the tantalizing aroma of coffee, Ron and Vicky didn't surface until nearly noon.

It was a bizarre weekend, to say the least. I was relieved to wave goodbye to them when they took me home and drove away Sunday evening.

There was a message on my answering machine from Drake. He said he missed me, and would call again later. His voice did sound wistful. Hearing from him completely undid all the self-talk I'd done over the weekend. My insides felt unsettled.

The next morning, I was back at my desk by the time Sally arrived.

"How was your weekend?" she asked, leaning against my doorframe with her mug of tea in hand.

My eyes rolled, although I swear I didn't intend them to, when I told her where I'd been.

"That good, huh." She didn't really look surprised.

"Oops, there goes the front door." We both heard the bell, which we have rigged up to sound in the back and the upstairs offices, at the same time. Sally headed toward the front.

About a minute later my intercom line buzzed.

"Sharon Ortega to see you." Sally's voice was neutral.

Sharon had obviously dressed without much attention to detail this morning. She wore a pair of black slacks and a white sweatshirt that showed gray smudges at the cuffs and elbows. Her breezy blond hair now hung limply, and her face without makeup was splotchy looking. She didn't waste any time on preliminaries once she was seated in the chair across from me.

"David is dead," she said flatly.

It took me a minute for me to associate that it was her restaurant business partner she was talking about. A variety of emotions flickered across her face and came out in her body language. Her face was puffy from crying, her eyes red rimmed. Her hands wouldn't stay still. She twisted her fingers around each other in a way that looked painful. Tension was evident in her arms and neck. Clearly, she was extremely shaken. Something told me she was scared.

I wished Ron were here. I couldn't imagine that Sharon was coming here to tell me this dire news as a friend. We weren't that close. If she intended to hire the firm to look into David's death, I would prefer that Ron be here to handle it. But he wasn't, so it looked like I was stuck.

"Tell me what happened, Sharon," I suggested, as gently as possible.

The quiet evenness in my voice unleashed a fresh flood of tears. It's like, when you're a kid, the cut doesn't hurt so bad until someone sympathizes with you. I handed her a box of Kleenex and let her take her time. Finally, the sniffles slowed down a bit.

"He was shot through the head," she said. "The police just called me about an hour ago. He was found in his car in the parking lot of a grocery store near his apartment. They think it was suicide."

"What do you think?"

"I'm not sure I *am* thinking right now," she said, taking a deep breath. "I don't believe it was suicide, at least I don't *want* to think so." She reached for a new tissue. "Charlie, I don't know what to believe."

"Had David been depressed recently? Any problems that you know of, personal or business?"

She was twisting one corner of the Kleenex between her thumb and index finger. "Not really depressed, no. We had a few business problems, like I told you the other day. Business had slowed down at the restaurant. We were both concerned about that. But, I always thought David had such a good grip on things. He was a doer, not a worrier. He was working on some new advertising to help bring people back."

"What about his personal life?"

"I don't know that much about it." She looked a little embarrassed. "We never talked about personal stuff very much. He was single, dated a lot. I never met any of his ladies. His parents are very devout Catholics. I remember meeting them when we had our grand opening. This is just going to devastate them." This started a whole new spasm of crying.

"What would you like me to do?" I asked after she calmed down a bit. "Are you hiring my firm to look into it?"

"Yes, I guess so. I don't know, Charlie. I don't have anything concrete to go on, but I can't believe David would kill himself."

"Why not let the police continue to investigate? If there are suspicious circumstances in the case, I'm sure they'll follow through with it."

She squirmed a little in her chair. "Well, there is one thing about this whole matter that involves me directly." She uncrossed her legs, and leaned toward me. "Charlie, please don't think badly of me for letting this be one of my first concerns. I mean, there hasn't even been a funeral yet, and I don't want you to get the wrong idea."

I waited, wondering what on earth she was getting at.

"When we started the business, David and I took out life insurance policies on each other. Well, really, the business paid for them. We each made the other partner beneficiary. Our thinking was, if something happened to one of us, the other would have money to keep the restaurant going."

"And?"

"And, the policies had a two-year suicide clause. If death was by suicide within the first two years, the policy wouldn't pay off. Oh, Charlie, I know that sounds horrible of me. I'd hate for anyone else to know I'm even bringing it up. But, without David, I'm going to have to hire someone else to handle the financial end of the business. We're operating on a shoestring as it is. I'll need that insurance money to stay in business."

# 5

She was in a tough spot, all right.

"I'll have to get some basic information about the case. I'm sure the police reports will have been filed by now. They may also be ordering an autopsy."

"I want to give you a retainer," she said. "How much would you need?"

I was torn. She was in a bind financially, and I felt guilty asking for anything. But, Ron and I had one basic rule of business. No allowances for personal friends. I couldn't do Sharon a favor at Ron's expense.

"Our rates are two-fifty a day, plus expenses. I should be able to find out enough within the first day to know whether it's worth proceeding any further. If we have to take it beyond that, we'll settle up then."

She wrote out a check for three hundred dollars on her personal account and signed our standard contract. I walked her to the front door and gave her a hug as she left.

Ron walked in the back door as I started up the stairs. I motioned him into my office, where he took the seat just vacated by Sharon. I filled him in on the situation, beginning with my meeting Sharon and David at the restaurant on Friday. He said he'd drive down to the police station and see if he could lay his hands on a copy of the police report. That's what I like about doing business with Ron. He's great at the legwork and he has contacts in all sorts of high places.

He was back an hour later with a whole folder of tidbits. The little bit Sharon had told me checked out. David Ruiz had been found, shot through the left temple, in his Porsche which was sitting in the parking lot of the Food City supermarket at the corner of San Mateo and Academy Road. One of the busiest intersections in town.

Ron had managed to make fairly decent photocopies of some of the crime scene photos. They showed the body draped across the center console, lower half in the driver's seat, upper half on the passenger side. The gun, a Smith & Wesson .357 Magnum, lay on the floor near his left hand.

I flipped through the sheets to a preliminary interview with the next of kin. Apparently, the parents had been too distraught to provide much information. Most of the answers had been provided by a cousin, Michael Mann. The transcribed interview read like a family squabble, with the elder Ruiz's insisting that David would never commit suicide, while Mann tried to tell the police that David had been worried about something recently.

"Taylor said at this point, they excused Mr. and Mrs. Ruiz from the room, so Mann could tell his story uninterrupted," Ron said, pointing to a spot partway down on the page.

"Kent Taylor? He's homicide, isn't he?"

"Yeah, but he says they've not officially ruled on the case yet. Right now they're just looking at all the possibilities."

I went on to read the rest of the cousin's statement. He told police that David Ruiz had been very upset about something recently. Mann thought it concerned business, but couldn't say for sure. David hadn't confided details to him. Mann had also told them that David was left handed.

"The case isn't closed yet, but Kent says they're leaning toward the suicide theory. It all looks like a pretty self-contained incident."

There were a few more photos of the scene, showing the parked car both close-up and at a distance. It sat at the outer fringes of the parking lot, not unusual for someone with an expensive car to do if they wanted to avoid getting their doors dinged up. Certainly not unusual enough to attract any attention at an all night grocery store.

Time of death had been established as sometime between ten and midnight, Saturday night. I tried to picture the location in my mind. There was a movie theater in the same shopping center, as well as a couple of fast food places. Surely, on a Saturday night there would have been a lot of activity, even that late. I'd think someone would have noticed a man sitting in an expensive car, putting a gun to his head. Even with traffic and horns and car radios blasting, probably *someone* would have heard the shot. The Porsche had apparently stayed in the lot overnight, until the police found it mid-morning on Sunday. I closed the file cover, but couldn't put the thoughts out of my mind.

"So, what did you think about Vicky?" Ron asked. "Isn't she nice?"

I didn't want to be cruel. "Ron, how old is she, really?"

"Twenty-four." His voice got defensive.

"Don't you think that's a bit young? What does she think about your three kids?"

"We haven't exactly gotten around to that, yet. I mean, she knows I have them. She just hasn't met them yet."

"Well, she sure seems to be crazy about you," I told him. I wanted to ask about her strange moodiness, whether she had anything to offer but sex, but when I tried to formulate the questions, I couldn't come up with a way to ask that didn't sound petty. Or worse yet, jealous.

He wasn't listening anyway. He said something about dictating a report for Sally to type before noon, and headed across the hall toward his own office. I couldn't sit still. I felt like we had to be doing something to earn the money Sharon had given us.

Rusty looked at me expectantly when he saw me pick up my keys and purse, but I told him he better stay here this time. He went back to his corner near the bay window. I buzzed Sally on the intercom and told her I'd be out for awhile. I went out the back door and started the Jeep. It was nearly noon and already hot. I switched on the air conditioner and rolled the windows down to blow the intense air out. From the weather report on the radio this morning, it sounded like the week-long warm trend was going to continue.

I wanted to take a look at David's desk at the restaurant, but hated to bother Sharon during the lunch hour. I decided to head across town to the scene of the . . . was it a crime? I meant to find out. I drove up Lomas to Second, and headed north until I came to the freeway. As I remembered, the shopping center where the police found David was located just off I-25 and San Mateo. I almost saw the off ramp too late, and some jerk in a dark blue Cadillac honked at me as I changed lanes in front of him. I slowed to the legal speed limit and let him stew as he was forced to follow along.

At this time of day the supermarket parking lot was packed. I wasn't sure exactly where the car had been parked, but judging from the photos I'd brought with me, I got a pretty good idea. There was one of those red and yellow free-standing photo booths in the middle of the parking lot with two blue

32

mailboxes next to it. I parked my Jeep and walked around until I could see the photo booth at approximately the same angle as the Xerox copy of the photograph showed. There was no indication now that a violent death had taken place here — no broken glass, no blood, no police tape or spectators. David's life had ended without fanfare.

I walked into the grocery store. The cold contrast of air-conditioning came as a relief after the hot sun outside. I found the manager in a little booth near the front.

"Excuse me, could I ask you a couple of questions?"

He looked up from a stack of papers he was rubber stamping. He was about forty, thin, with black hair and old acne scars. He had a smudge of ink across his chin, but I thought it best not to mention it. His name was Alvin Rodriguez according to his name badge.

"Sure. How can I help you?"

"Were you working Saturday night? Between ten and twelve p.m.?"

"No, the night manager would have been here then."

"How about any of the other employees? Checkers, or anyone who's here now that might have been working then."

"I don't think so," he said. "Why?"

I gave him my business card, which he dropped on his desk without a glance. Sighing, he said, "I'll check the schedule."

He pulled a white sheet of paper from a drawer down near his knees. I got a glimpse of a very complicated looking chart. He looked it over quickly, running his index finger down the rows, one by one.

"No, I didn't think so. You want to talk to the night people, you'll have to come back at night."

What a wealth of information this guy was. I guess I should have figured that out myself. I left the store feeling unsatisfied. I supposed the same story would hold true if I were to check the other businesses in the center. I would just have to come back in the evening to see if I could learn anything.

It was after one o'clock, and I was starving. The french fry scent from the nearby McDonald's was beginning to make me salivate. I pulled through the drive-up and got some chicken nuggets that I scarfed down without sauce. I figured it might be late enough now that I could catch Sharon and try to gain access to David's desk.

I had just pulled out of the shopping center, heading in the direction of the freeway on-ramp, when I noticed that the Porsche dealership was right here. On impulse, I swerved in and took the first open parking space I saw. I lifted the cover on the police file once more, to get a picture of David's car firmly in my mind. I spotted one just like it and walked toward it.

I had not quite circled the car once before a salesman was at my side.

"Beautiful car, isn't it?" he asked smoothly. Despite the heat, his white shirt was still crisp, his tie perfectly knotted. He had, however, removed his suit jacket. His blond hair was expensively cut and his flat nails were buffed to a shine. He looked to be in his late twenties.

"Yes," I answered, "I was just admiring it. Could I sit in it?"

"Go ahead," he said, pulling the door open, and standing back graciously.

The leather seats felt like they'd been custom made for my rear end. A roll of padding lined the outside edges of the seat, rising up on either side of my hips just enough to make me feel secure. At a hundred twenty pounds, I consider myself to be of about average build. Even so, I wasn't sure how anyone much larger would manage these seats. They were definitely built for slim people. The rest of the interior was just as comfortable. The gear shift was right at my fingertips. A padded console divided the space between driver and passenger, giving a nice place to rest my forearm. The instruments were basic and easy to look at.

I pulled the door shut and put my hands on the wheel like I was driving. My eyes scanned the instruments — everything okay there. Now I reached for the gear shift with my right hand. Ready, clutch, okay. Yes! I could see myself zooming past other cars like they were standing still. The announcer's voice was clear and triumphant. Yes, folks, in the final laps of the Indianapolis 500, Charlie Parker easily takes the checkered flag.

The door opened just then, abruptly bringing me back to Albuquerque. I guess the salesman was nervous, not being able to talk to me.

"What do you think? Want to take it for a test drive?"

I had to make a conscious effort not to drool.

"I better not, not this time." I reminded myself that I had a job to do. This is purely research, I repeated internally. You cannot afford this car. You must get back to work. My inner voice kept working at me, but it had to do some imaginary tugging at the back of my collar to get me out of the Porsche and back to my own set of wheels.

# 6

Still daydreaming twenty-five minutes later, I walked into Sharon's restaurant. She was making a gallant effort at conducting business as usual, but I could tell it was a strain. The waiters stood around like they weren't sure what to do next.

"We had a good sized lunch crowd today," Sharon told me, as she showed me to David's office. "Morbid curiosity, I think. There was a long story and a picture of David in this morning's *Journal*."

David's office consisted of a small room near the back alley door, which had been constructed by setting up some hasty partitions of two-by-fours and nailing drywall over them. The door had a lock, but even I could have easily gotten past it. Inside, an old metal desk took up most of the space. Behind it, some one-by-twelve boards laid across metal brackets formed a set of shelves, which were laden to the point of sagging. There were stacks of computer printouts, file folders, and miscellaneous papers, along with books on restaurant management and computer operation manuals. Unframed snapshots of David, each with a different woman on his arm, were propped against the books. The women all had dark eyes and lots of hair, like he'd gone through the roster of a modeling school to find his dates.

A personal computer sat to one side of the desk. The remaining space was cluttered with calculator, stapler, and a shallow dish of paper clips just waiting to be tipped over. A mug, half full of oily looking coffee, sat perilously near the computer keyboard. On the side of the mug was a cartoon showing a haggard looking office worker receiving a pink slip, and the saying "Go Ahead, Make My Day."

Scattered across the top of several layers of file folders, and ripped-open envelopes were a handful of phone messages, the kind written on pink forms.

"I take it these came in before Saturday," I commented to Sharon.

Her brows pulled together in the center as she looked them over.

"Heavens, yes," she said. "Look at the dates on some of them. Looks like they've been here for weeks."

"I wonder if that means David never returned the calls."

"I really couldn't say, but as you can see, he was a real pack-rat. It's very possible that he returned the calls, but kept the messages anyway." She looked at me and shrugged. "I just don't know."

"Has anyone else been in here since Friday?"

"No. I half expected the police to stop by, but they haven't."

"Do you mind if I spend a little time in here? I won't take anything with me unless I check it out with you first."

"Go right ahead, Charlie. Do whatever you need to. I just want answers." She picked up the coffee mug and took it with her.

I began by sorting the phone messages. Some of them were almost two months old. A couple had notes scribbled in the margins in straight masculine looking writing. I assumed David had returned those and had made the notes. Three of the messages were from a Mr. Tom McDonald with the IRS. None of those had notes in David's writing.

I pulled out the small spiral notebook I always keep in my purse and copied the names, phone numbers, and all notes from the phone messages. If the police discarded the suicide theory and opened this as a murder investigation, they would certainly search this office. I didn't want to face obstruction of justice charges by removing anything that could potentially be important. But, that didn't mean I wasn't ready to glean any and all information I could.

Systematically, I went through each of the drawers, which turned out to be about as organized as the desktop. The farther I dug, the more I began to wonder about David's competence as the financial wizard of the business. Accountants are people, and as in every other walk of life, they are all different. But one thing I've noticed almost universally (at least among the ones I know) is that their records are organized. Without organization, without being able to put one's hands on any certain piece of paper at any time, an accountant would be hopelessly lost. David's desk looked pretty hopeless.

I had to resist the temptation to straighten the files and move things around. After all, I was here to find clues, if any existed, to prove that David had not committed suicide, not to revamp his office procedures. On the surface anyway there was nothing to indicate that David hadn't left here on Friday night with every intention of being back at this desk Monday morning.

I switched on the PC, wondering if the files there might yield some new clues. Checking the root directory, I saw that the most recent entries to his accounting program had been made just after the first of the month, more than two weeks ago. His word processor, though, had been updated just last Friday. I changed to that directory and opened the program. Its sub-directory showed that two files had been worked on that day. I pulled up the first one. It was a letter to one of their food suppliers regarding a past due bill. David was asking the supplier to extend credit an extra month past their usual terms. The second document was a similar letter to the bank. Sounded like David was having to do some sweet-talking to shuffle money where it was needed.

I riffled again through the papers covering the top of the desk. Quite a few of them were bills, some with past due notices. None had yet reached the Final stage and, for the most part, the messages were courteous but firm. It was obvious David was getting some pressure, but enough to drive him to suicide? I wouldn't think so.

Nothing else on the computer looked urgent or even especially timely so I switched it off. I pulled open the center lap drawer on the desk. Its contents were almost in worse shape than the rest of the small office. He had one of those little divided trays that is supposed to provide a place for everything, but the drawer was so jammed that the tray couldn't even rest flat on the bottom. Papers, pens, clips, little notepads, and a variety of junk, including a wadded up hamburger wrapper, all came at me as I pulled at the drawer. This was unbearable.

I began to pull out handfuls of stuff, attempting to locate the bottom of the mess. Finally, I had it down to one layer. The heaviest objects had settled to the bottom, among them a keyring. I picked it up. There were only four keys on it. Three were obviously for doors — his home, his office, and something else? I could ask Sharon. The fourth was a safe deposit box key.

*39*

Setting the keyring aside, I replaced the papers I had
pulled out, one at a time. I glanced at each one, wondering if
I would find a suicide note. Nothing there. The drawer closed
a little easier than it had opened. I picked up the keys, and
tried them one at a time, until I ascertained that one fit the
door to the office, and another fit the restaurant's back door
to the alley. Presumably, the front door would be keyed the
same. That left one more door key, which was most likely his
home, and the safe deposit key.

I felt like I'd checked what I could here. Without delving
into the books or searching each of his files page by page, I
couldn't find anything that I thought would drive a man to kill
himself.

Sharon was at the cash register, closing out the sales for
the day. She brightened a bit when she saw me.

"We did better than I expected today," she said. "How
about you? Find anything?"

"No, not really," I said. I showed her the keyring. "Was this
a spare set of keys David kept?"

She looked at them. "I guess so. His regular keyring had
a little plastic thing attached that said 'I heart NM'. You know
the kind. His little sister had given it to him." She took the
keys from me and flipped through them. "These two are for
the restaurant," she said, confirming what I'd already tested.
"I don't know about the others."

"His house, maybe?"

"Probably. He lived in those apartments on Academy Road
— I can't think of the name, but they're just up the street from
the Food City grocery store."

"Mind if I take those?" I asked.

She handed the keys back. "Like I said, I just want to find
out the truth."

Back on the road, I contemplated what I was doing. I
wasn't sure how the police would feel about me snooping

around in David's apartment. But, if I didn't remove anything— Besides that, I justified, they had probably already
searched the place themselves. If there was a suicide note, I
felt sure the police or David's family would have recovered it
by now. If not, then what harm would I be doing?

# 7

The Jeep headed back across town for the second time this afternoon. A hot pale blue sky reflected heat waves off the freeway. Bright chrome shining off other cars struck my eyes. The traffic became a clog at the Big I, where Interstate 40 bisects Interstate 25. I slowed to twenty-five miles an hour, thinking about the weekend I'd just spent in the cool deserted mountains. Slowly, the pace picked up a little. I worked my way over to the right, watching for the San Mateo exit.

I found the apartment complex Sharon had mentioned. The place consisted of five or six frame stucco buildings styled and colored to look like adobe. According to the mailboxes, D. Ruiz was in apartment A48. It took me a few minutes of wandering around to figure out the numbering system and locate the right one.

The key slid into the well-worn lock with hardly a whisper. I used a scarf over my hand to turn the knob, just in case the police would come by later for fingerprints. The apartment looked like David had just stepped out to do a quick errand. The drapes were drawn; a lamp in the living room still burned. A TV schedule was open on the coffee table to Saturday's date, with the remote control lying on top of it. The furniture all looked new, and expensive. David's taste ran to the modern — leather, chrome, and glass. His stereo system was the latest, with enough controls and buttons to operate a space shuttle. Nothing in the room looked more than six months old.

A sack from Burger King lay on its side on the breakfast bar, a hamburger wrapper spread flat beside it. The remains of the hamburger, a sprinkling of sesame seeds and a few shreds of dried up lettuce, were scattered about the paper surface. A puddle of ketchup, dried now to the color of blood, held one corner of the paper down, and three shriveled french fries lay in their cardboard container. A Coors can, which proved to be about two-thirds empty, stood nearby. The wooden bar chair in front of the food remains was swiveled toward the living room, like David had just gotten up to go to the bathroom and would be right back.

It was an eerie feeling, walking into the just-vacated place. It wouldn't have surprised me a bit if David had emerged that minute from the bedroom. I found myself tip-toeing around. The apartment was relatively neat, compared to David's office. There was a dirty coffee mug in the kitchen sink, and the refrigerator revealed three cold cans of Coors and a cardboard box from Pizza Hut. David's grocery bill must have been very reasonable.

In the bathroom, the light was still on. A shirt tail trailed out from under the clothes hamper lid, and his towel had been stuffed over the towel bar in a wad. The medicine cabinet held an assortment of shaving paraphernalia and dental care products. A pack of twenty-four condoms was open. There were only two left. I didn't see any drugs, prescription or the other kind. Nothing out of the ordinary.

The bedroom was dim with the drapes closed. I hit the wall switch, which turned on a bedside lamp. The bed was unmade, a pair of dress shoes sat on the floor, and a suit jacket lay draped over a chair. A small desk stood in the corner, obviously not as heavily used as his desk at the restaurant. In the top drawer I found a coupon book for car payments. Glancing into it made me glad I hadn't purchased that Porsche earlier. He had also racked up a sizeable bill at one of the priciest mens clothing stores in town.

I hadn't seen a trace of a suicide note, and I was beginning to feel nervous about being here. For all I knew, the police or David's family members could come traipsing in just any time now. In fact, it surprised me that I was apparently the first on the scene. Still using my scarf, I made sure I left everything as I'd found it, then slipped out the front door.

It was getting close to five o'clock, and the traffic was picking up. I wasn't eager to get into the mess on the freeway, but I didn't have much choice. I pulled into a convenience store, and bought a copy of the evening paper before heading south. By the time I got back to the office, everyone else was long gone, and Rusty looked anxious. I reassured him that I had intended all along to come back for him.

I checked the answering machine and my desk. No messages either place. I dialed Ron's number, but there was no answer. Rusty and I headed for home. He got a scoop of dry food, and I had a can of chicken noodle soup for dinner. I felt let down that day one of my investigating hadn't netted much for Sharon. I thought about calling her at home, but didn't know what I'd say, so I didn't. Rusty and I both were ready for the sack by nine.

At six a.m. my eyes were suddenly wide open. The penalty, I guess, for going to bed so early. I got up, made coffee, and read last night's paper while chewing on a bowl of granola and dried fruit. In the obituaries, I noticed that David's funeral would be this morning at ten.

I should probably go, although I absolutely detest funerals. It's an old phobia, traceable to the fact that I had to attend both my parent's when I was only sixteen. As if the shock of someone's death isn't bad enough, just about the time we're coming to grips with it, society demands that we hold this ceremony to rip the painful wound open again. The only reason I even considered going this morning was because I didn't really know David, and could, therefore, stay emotionally detached. That's what I told myself, anyway.

Actually, I hoped to get a clearer picture of David's family situation. Seeing them all together might give me some further insights into the man himself. Plus, I could see Sharon again and let her know what I had, or rather hadn't, found. She could tell me whether she wanted me to keep trying.

Staring into my closet proved to be an unsatisfying venture. The weather was still above normal for late May, and I didn't seem to own anything in a subdued color that wasn't also heavy. I finally settled on a navy blue linen suit and white blouse. If the funeral home was air conditioned, I'd be okay. If we went to the cemetery, the jacket would probably have to go.

My hair felt heavy and hot against my neck. It's thick and just below shoulder length, and every summer I swear I'll get it all cut off. I thought about wearing it up today, but remembered that I still had a centipede-like adornment of stitches at the base of the hairline. I'd need to get an appointment to have them taken out.

Meanwhile the house was hot and I was getting irritable. I really needed to get my air conditioner hooked up. I should have made arrangements for that before I ever left on vacation. I pulled the yellow pages out of my nightstand drawer, and looked for the name of the guy who'd done it last year.

The secretary who answered said that he was solidly booked until next week. Would that be soon enough? I told her I guessed it would; what choice did I have?

I also dialed the office, and told Sally my plans for the morning. If there were any calls for me, I could be reached at home until nine-thirty, or I'd be in the office by noon.

I showered, put on the suit, and did a quick makeup job. All this took about fifteen minutes, but still, it's major primping for me. I'm usually a jeans and T-shirt/sweatshirt/wool sweater kind of person, depending on the season. I do minimal makeup, and the dressy version varies from the everyday version only with the addition of a few extra swipes of blusher, and *maybe* eyeshadow. Not today. I didn't want any weird colors caking up in the sweaty places I could already feel forming on my face.

Rusty wasn't thrilled about staying home alone, but hey, we can't always have our way. I was wearing a suit and high heels, so I figured he could give a little, too.

I drove north on Rio Grande Boulevard to I-40, heading toward the same funeral home where I'd last seen my parents.

# 8

Nothing had changed. Somber men in dark suits stood near the doors, speaking in their same low tones, ushering people to the proper places. The flowers still smelled overly sweet and the organ played the same music it had almost fifteen years ago. The casket at the front became fuzzy as I stared at it, the image splitting and becoming two, and I had to squeeze my eyes shut for a moment to make the memory go away.

Sharon was seated alone in the fourth row, and I slipped into the pew beside her. Her eyes were red when she glanced up at me. She took my hand and clutched it briefly. I felt my eyes begin to sting, not so much for the passing of David, whom I'd barely met, but for the loss it represented to her.

As the priest finished his ceremonial ministerings, and one of David's brothers stood up to deliver the eulogy, I found myself getting caught up in the family's grief. I didn't want that to happen. I forced myself to tune out the words. Instead, I concentrated on assessing the players in the sad drama.

David's parents sat beside each other in the front row, huddling together, locking out the rest of the world in their grief. A small elderly woman hunched next to Mrs. Ruiz, her face hidden by a black lace mantilla. Her gnarled fingers worked systematically at a set of rosary beads. Behind the three of them was a row apparently comprised of the brothers and sisters — three women and two men, all in their twenties and thirties.

Across the aisle from the immediate family, were three rows set aside for other family. Judging by their assorted ages, I guessed them to be the aunts, uncles, cousins, nieces and nephews.

Sharon had caught my line of sight. "The good-looking man on the end is David's cousin, Michael Mann. I've met some of the others, but can't remember who's who."

Michael Mann was the one who had given his statement to the police. I would be interested in talking to him later, if I got the chance.

Outside, the sun was hotter than before, or perhaps it was the contrast with the overly air-conditioned room that I noticed. My fingers were frigid. The dry desert air had a cleansing effect as I breathed deeply, getting the cloying scent of the flowers out of my nostrils.

"There will be a short graveside service," Sharon said, "then we're invited to the Ruiz's home. You want to come?"

"I'd like to meet the family," I told her. "I know this isn't the time for questions, but I might be able to pick up something."

I hung back at the fringes during the graveside service, partly out of distaste for the whole ceremony and partly to watch the others participate. Sharon had offered to let me ride with her, but I didn't want to be stuck without an escape hatch. I followed her in my car to the Ruiz home.

The place was way down in the south valley, in an area where a man's riches are apparently judged by the land he holds and the number of children he produces. The homes aren't anything to get excited about. The Ruiz place had started out as a small flat-roofed cinderblock house, stuccoed pinkish-tan. Subsequent additions had been stuccoed separately, each job getting pinker and pinker, until the most recent, an angular affair sticking out the back, was almost strawberry — like a child's birthday cake gone wrong.

Cars already lined both sides of the narrow dirt road by the time Sharon and I arrived. I pulled into a spot far back in the line, leaving myself plenty of room. Groups of teens clustered in the narrow band of shade at the front of the house, eating off paper plates and balancing Coke cans. Younger children, freed from the heavy religious atmosphere, shrieked and ran across the front lawn. Sharon and I walked inside together.

The small living room was jammed with people, and the overflow had already gone over into the dining room and presumably the kitchen as well. It was like a sauna inside. English and Spanish phrases floated through the air, blending until I had a hard time distinguishing either. I spotted the old grandmother in a narrow wooden rocking chair beside a vintage 60s Danish modern TV set. She had a paper plate balanced precariously on her lap, and was picking the last bits of crispy off a chicken bone. Her lace mantilla was now draped around her shoulders and I could see that her hair was steel gray. Her deeply lined face suggested a life spent working outside in the sun.

A knot of people who had been standing just inside the doorway pushed past us to get outside. Their departure cleared the room considerably. The small room was over-furnished as it was. Two couches faced each other from opposite walls. Both were covered with crocheted yarn afghans in brilliant rainbow colors. The lower edges of the couches exposed peeling orange vinyl. Cone-shaped metal legs, tipped with flat metal feet, showed underneath. The vinyl arms were cracked, with small bits of stuffing poking out randomly. A hard-looking recliner chair covered in brown vinyl the color of old beef jerky stood in an awkward spot in the middle of the room. Apparently, no one wanted to sit there because of constant jostling by anyone who tried to get around it. A small plastic Jesus stood next to the rabbit ears antenna on the TV set, and a large gilt-framed portrait of the Savior took up most of one wall above the gaudier of the two couches. I tried to imagine the person who, somewhere back in history, would have walked into a furniture store and said, "I love this furniture," and plunked down hard-earned money to buy it.

I thought the woman seated in the center of the nearest afghan-covered couch was Mrs. Ruiz, but I couldn't be sure, since I'd only seen the back of her head during the service.

Three men stood in the wide arched opening to the dining room, and Sharon steered me toward them.

"Charlie, I'd like you to meet Mr. Ruiz," she said, indicating the eldest of the three. "And, this is Michael Mann, and David's brother, Bobby Ruiz."

David's father looked like a man who had spent his life in the sun. A small man at about five foot six, he had broad shoulders and tan forearms. His dark face was deeply lined, his black eyes had permanent squint marks that radiated clear to his hairline at the sides. His forehead had a flat strip across it where his hatband had shaped it for life. He had removed his jacket and tie, but even with the sleeves of his dress shirt rolled up, he seemed overdressed. He would be more natural in faded Levis and plaid work shirt.

I made polite sounds, along with an appropriately sympathetic face.

"Charlie is the woman I've hired to investigate David's death," she told the men.

"Good, good." Mr. Ruiz was the first to speak up. "My David would never have killed himself. He knew suicide is a mortal sin. He would never do it." He patted my arm. "You will find out."

I smiled and assured him I would try. "I know you don't want to answer questions now," I said, "but I'd like to talk further with you. Could I plan to come back tomorrow?"

He nodded. "You will want to speak with Bernice, also. Maybe tomorrow she will be feeling better."

I turned to speak to Michael Mann, but he had left the group.

Sharon touched my arm. "Want some food? There's plenty."

I felt funny joining in the social aspects of what was meant to be a family time of sorrow, but Sharon propelled me toward the dining table without another word. She was right about the quantity of food. Pans and covered dishes had been set out, heaped with about three times as much as it would take to feed the crowd. I helped myself to guacamole dip, home-made tamales, enchilada casserole, and three different salads. I was scanning the area, looking for flatware and a napkin, when I happened to glance toward the kitchen.

Through the open kitchen door, I saw a man and woman standing near the stove. They stood not more than six inches apart, and were having a rather intense-looking conversation. She reached up a couple of times and touched the side of his face lovingly. They embraced, exchanging a kiss capable of causing tonsilar damage. She turned to leave by the back door. The woman was Vicky.

# 9

"Here, Charlie." Sharon handed me a paper napkin wrapped around a plastic fork and knife.

When I glanced back up, Vicky was gone.

I wanted to run after her, confront her, and scream out what a lousy little slut I thought she was. Charlie Parker to the rescue, saving her brother from the clutches of a scheming vixen. "Charlie?" Sharon was staring at me. "Shall we find a spot to sit down?"

I nodded numbly. We walked through the dining room to the back, where a large room had caught the crowd overflow. The den had missed out on the good furniture. A ping-pong table filled the center of the room. The perimeter had been lined with metal folding chairs, the kind you might borrow for such an occasion from the church recreation hall. Sharon and I found two, and took them, perching our paper plates on our knees. I hoped this was not the brand they showed on television where greasy food leaked through as an example of which kind not to buy.

Chewing on tamales and listening to Sharon talk gave me time to cool down over seeing Vicky. It really was none of my business anyway. As far as I knew, she and Ron hadn't made any type of exclusivity promises to each other. I wouldn't say anything to her but I wrestled with whether or not I should drop a hint to Ron. I decided not.

"Hello, I am Mrs. Padilla." The middle-aged woman sitting next to me turned to introduce herself. "Esther. Richard and I live next door," she said. "We have known David since he was born."

I wiped my hand on my napkin, ready to shake hers, but she kept her hands busy with her plate. She looked much like Mrs. Ruiz, two Hispanic women, wives of farmers, who had raised their children side by side. I asked her if they were possibly related.

"No, we aren't," she said, "but our daughters are all the same age. They act like sisters."

I was through with my food and ready to get out of there. I made what I hoped were polite sounding excuses to Mrs. Padilla, and to Sharon, before I bolted for the door. Michael Mann stood just outside the front door, almost like he was waiting for me.

"Ms. Parker? Could we talk for a minute?"

"Sure." We stepped around the far side of the house, where a carport created a welcome shady spot. It was also out of earshot of the open windows.

"I wanted to speak with you inside," he said, "but with Uncle Ralph right there, well . . . I couldn't speak very freely."

I waited, remembering that he had disagreed with the Ruiz's during the police interview. For the first time, I really noticed him. Michael was a little younger than David, about twenty-four, I'd guess. He was right at six feet tall, slim, with

Eric Estrada-like handsomeness. His face was smooth, with a couple of dimples in just the right places. His dark, slightly wavy hair was trim and neat. He had removed the jacket he'd worn to the funeral, and rolled up the sleeves of his white shirt. Fine dark hair grew thick on his forearms. He had a gold band on his left ring finger.

"My wife says I should leave this alone," he told me. "Said the family is already upset enough as it is. But something bothers me about David's death. Sharon told me you're investigating it, so I think you should know this. Uncle Ralph closes his eyes to a lot of things. I think David had been upset about something recently."

"Depressed?"

He thought about it for a few seconds, searching for the right word. "No, I'd say more like scared. Nervous. Something was really worrying him."

"When was the last time you saw David?" I asked.

"Friday night after work. We stopped off and had a couple of beers."

"Did he talk about it?"

"Nothing specific. I thought it might be money. He said something about the bills really piling up."

I thought about the payment book I'd seen for his Porsche. And the rent on his apartment had to be on the pricey side. And then there were the past-dues I'd seen in his office. Maybe Michael was right.

"Anything else you can think of?"

"Not really," he said. "I just wanted you to know that all this 'mortal sin' stuff wouldn't have meant shit to David. I mean, his parents are all religious and everything, but not David. No matter what his mother and father say, he just wasn't into that stuff."

I dug around through my purse, and handed him my card. "I appreciate the information. If you think of something later, could you call me?"

He stared at the card for a minute, as though something about it was familiar to him, but he said nothing. Stuck the card in his wallet and pulled out a card of his own.

He was a commercial real estate specialist with one of the largest firms in town, I noticed. Now I knew where I'd heard the name before. There had been a recent article in the paper about how he'd closed the deal on a new twenty million dollar shopping center project. I said goodbye and thanked him.

I left him standing there under the carport. I was one of the first to leave, I guess, because the rows of cars on the road hadn't thinned out at all. After much maneuvering and backing up, I managed to get headed back toward the interstate and my office.

Sally was getting ready to leave for the day. Ron looked relieved that I had arrived to take over the phones. I half-jokingly asked what was the matter with *his* arm. He didn't bother me the rest of the afternoon, while I caught up on my billing. I remembered to put a call in to Dr. Casper. Linda was with a patient but her receptionist told me to come by the next afternoon, anytime. That's what I like about going to a doctor who isn't well known yet.

About four o'clock, Ron peeked into my office.

"Did you bill your friend anything in the David Ruiz case?" he asked.

"One day, so far."

"I talked to Kent Taylor this afternoon," he said, leaning on the doorjamb. "He's about to meet with the D.A. and medical examiner on this. Says he's pretty sure they'll rule suicide."

I thought about the funeral this morning and felt myself slump. "I don't know, Ron. A lot of people who knew this guy swear he wouldn't have done it."

"Like his parents."

"Well, yeah." I had to remember his own cousin seemed to feel it was possible.

"We're always blind about those we love," he said.

I was reminded of what I'd seen in the Ruiz's kitchen.

"Yeah. Well, I'll talk to Sharon about it, and see if she wants us to continue."

"We won't get much police cooperation."

"Do we ever? I went to David's apartment yesterday. The place looked like he'd just stepped out for a few minutes. Does a guy pay for a hamburger, sit down and eat it, then go out and shoot himself? And why at the grocery store? He could have done it at home in the comfort of his own bed, for chrissakes."

"Why would anyone else kill him in such a public place, though," Ron said. "If somebody lured him out to meet them in the parking lot, why wouldn't they choose a quieter place? Somewhere out on the west mesa, or some little mountain road in the canyon?"

"Maybe it was someone David was afraid of, someone he would only agree to meet in a very public place."

He shuffled a little to concede that I might have a point. "Look, Charlie, I just don't have the time to work on it," he said. "These other two cases are keeping me hopping. Mrs. Boyd wants me to wrap up her evidence soon, and I don't have it yet. Surveillance work just drives me nuts."

I knew what he meant and didn't offer to trade places with him.

"I think I'll do a little more snooping around," I said, "with or without Sharon's okay, just to learn a bit more. Right now, I'm going home to get out of these shoes."

Ron went back to his desk while I signed off my computer and quickly updated my backup disk.

At home, Rusty was overjoyed to see me. I let him out in the backyard while I changed into jeans, a T-shirt, and tennies. I didn't have to ask twice if he'd like to go for a ride. I hoped I could catch some of the night crew at Food City who might have been working Saturday night.

The sun, fiery orange, was low in the sky by the time we headed out. The temperature was still well over ninety but it's a dry heat. I switched on the Jeep's air conditioning anyway. Rusty's tongue was hanging out to one side after his romp in the back yard and he gratefully collapsed in front of the cold air vents. The freeway traffic was light now, the go-home rush all gone home, and we had reached the San Mateo off-ramp within fifteen minutes.

I parked at the side of the large grocery store, where the shadows had already lengthened. With the windows rolled most of the way down, a cool breeze came through. It wasn't unpleasant, despite the outside temperature. I focused my attention toward the front of the store, watching the traffic patterns, trying to get a feel for the place. The small strip center was shaped like an L, which took up two sides of the square property, the other two sides being major streets. The grocery store anchored the long end of the L, while a small four-screen movie theater served the same function at the opposite end. In between, a neighborhood bar and an exercise club drew most of the traffic. The few other stores, an office supply, a beauty shop, and a book store among them, had already closed. Three fast food places, neatly staked out along the two streets, enjoyed a steady flow of traffic through their drive-up lanes.

In my glove compartment I located my small pair of binoculars. With them I could read the marquee and see that the movies were timed so that something was beginning or ending about every fifteen minutes all evening long. There would be a steady stream of traffic in and out of there until nearly midnight. On Saturday night I imagined the flow would be even heavier.

Generally, the entire center was constant motion. A car sitting out in the middle somewhere, even occupied, would draw little, if any, attention. Amidst the constant din of traffic, horns, shouts, not to mention the interruptions of boom-box radios and the occasional siren from the fire station three blocks away, a single gunshot might well go unnoticed. In many ways, if someone wanted to blow David Ruiz away, this was a very good place to do it.

I left Rusty in the Jeep, promising to not stay away too long.

I was in a not-too-hopeful mood as I approached the night manager of Food City. He was a slight man with pale brown hair and many freckles. His name tag said he was J. Sanders. I found him sacking groceries for a customer while telling the checker to page somebody named Jason to the front immediately.

I waited at the side until a sullen looking sixteen-year-old appeared, dragging his feet. Mr. Sanders flashed him a look that he probably wouldn't have wanted the customers to see. I lagged a discrete distance behind until he had settled into his booth. When I approached, he still looked a bit irritated. I took my chances.

"Mr. Sanders? I wonder if I might ask you a couple of questions?"

He appeared relieved that I wasn't one of his employees. He told me that most of tonight's crew were the same ones working Saturday night. They had already been questioned by the police, and as far as he knew, no one had seen anything. He pointed out that, from inside the store, it was nearly impossible to monitor the parking lot. Just a month ago, he told me, a woman's purse had been snatched right on the sidewalk outside, and no one inside had noticed a thing until she ran through the door screaming.

"Do the sackers carry groceries out to the customer's cars?"

I asked.

"If we're not short handed they do. If the customer wants it."

"Do you mind if I ask that young man a question or two?" I asked, indicating Jason.

He didn't look too pleased. "Make them quick. That kid likes any excuse to duck out on a little work."

I figured a sixteen year old boy would have been the most likely one to spot a brand new Porsche in the parking lot. If he was in and out of the store throughout the evening, he might have noticed something funny going on.

I waited discreetly until Jason had carried out a customer's groceries before I approached him. He was over six feet tall, height he had probably attained in the last six months. He didn't look entirely comfortable with it yet. He wore baggy pants, a touch too short, and his camouflage T-shirt hung below his fingertips.

"Jason?"

He looked up immediately, but took his time sizing me up before he acknowledged me. He had straight blond hair, cut in a popular style that would have gotten him laughed off campus in my day.

"Yeah?"

"Mr. Sanders said it would be okay if I asked you a couple more questions about Saturday night."

He glanced nervously at the manager's booth.

"Did you notice a red Porsche in the parking lot that night?"

"Yeah, it was cool. A 944 Turbo."

"Did you walk out to it, to check it out?"

He shook his head. "Naw, it was way the hell out there."

"See a guy in it?"

"Uh, yeah, there was some dude in it at first. After awhile I didn't see him though. You know, I just thought he went in the movies or somethin'."

"What about when you got off work?"

"Uh, yeah, the car was still there."

"And you weren't tempted to walk over and get a better look at it as you left?"

"I didn't get the chance," he said. He shuffled a little, looking discomfited. "My dad picked me up right outside the front door here."

Ah, the ultimate embarrassment. Sixteen years old, and no wheels of his own. Being chauffeured around by Dad is second only in humiliation to being driven by Mom. A boy's worst nightmare.

I thanked him and went back out to the Jeep. Rusty was panting heavily, poor thing. I pulled through the drive-up lane of one of the fast food places where they charged me sixty-five cents for a cup of ice. Steep, but Rusty was grateful. He chomped on the cubes while I headed back home.

I pictured David sitting in his car in the parking lot. What had been going through his mind? I remembered the messages on his desk from the IRS. Perhaps Michael was right about his cousin. Maybe David's money problems had become serious.

# 10

My mainstay dinner at least two or three nights a week is usually Pedro's sour cream chicken enchiladas. I'd been home five whole days now without having them. Something was seriously wrong.

The small adobe building on the fringes of Old Town manages to avoid most of the tourist trade. Probably because it just doesn't look like much. The small wooden sign, painted blue, with the single word, PEDRO'S, might mislead some into thinking the place is a private house. Indeed, except for the five parking spaces out front, it probably could be. I pulled into a space just outside the door.

There was only one other vehicle in evidence, a dust-covered pickup truck belonging to an old-timer named Manny. Manny is there even more often than I, and he boasts being able to take his chile as hot as it comes. Once in awhile an unfamiliar gringo will wander in and actually be stupid enough to get caught up in a bet with Manny. Manny may not have become exactly rich this way, but his little diversion has managed to keep him well supplied with tequila shooters. Pedro once told me that Manny is somewhere around sixty, with the insides of a teenager.

When Rusty saw where we were, he jumped across my lap and out the open door on my side. By the time I had rolled up the windows and checked the locks, he had nosed open Pedro's warped screen door, and walked right on in. Pedro was scratching Rusty's ears and fussing over him by the time I got inside.

"Concha!" he called. "Concha, you better come here. There is some stranger walking in our door."

Concha came out of the kitchen, wiping her hands on a towel, and looked me up and down. "Eee, I think you're right. Who is this girl? Have we seen this one before?"

I felt guilty that I hadn't brought them anything from Hawaii. I could have picked up an extra tin of macadamia nuts or something, although Pedro is usually suspicious of all foods that don't come from his own kitchen.

They teased me about staying away too long, but they both hugged me at the same time. Manny sat at his usual table in the corner, watching the little reunion, his dark brown face with its perpetual sprinkling of white whiskers remaining placid. I gave a little wave in his direction. He kept on chewing, raising his chin briefly toward me in the way of a greeting.

"You look good, little girl," Concha said, holding me at arm's length.

She's always called me "little girl," ever since I really was a little girl, coming here with my dad. It seems a bit silly now, since she stands all of four feet ten inches. At five-six, I feel like I tower over her. She makes up for it in the width department, though, her roundness giving her the overall shape of a penguin. Her smooth flat face remains unwrinkled, belying the fact that she must be in her mid-fifties.

Pedro, on the other hand, is a skinny little rail. He always wears white. White shirt, white pants, white apron, and in winter, a funny little white knit cap that he pulls on over his graying hair. He has lots of kindly wrinkles around his eyes and deep smile lines on either side of his mouth. His hands are beginning to warp with arthritis. He had stepped behind the bar and returned now with a margarita for me.

"This one on the house," he said, "to welcome you home."

I wanted to protest, knowing they barely scratched out a living from the little place but I knew it would offend him. Pedro is one of those generous souls who is most happy when he can do a favor for someone else.

He continued to fuss around me, bringing flatware and napkin, making a show of dusting the crumbs off my chair. Like Manny, I have my regular table here. Mine is tucked into a corner on the opposite side of the room from his. That's not saying much. The place is only about forty feet square, and at least half of that is taken up by the bar, a heavy wooden carved affair from Mexico. That leaves space for only six tables. Pedro suggested this one to me because it's far enough into the shadowy corner that Rusty can lie down beside my chair without attracting the attention of anyone who's not used to seeing a dog in a food establishment.

The margarita was perfection. Lightly foamy on top, the rim of the glass crisp with salt crystals. My tongue puckered slightly as I took the first sip. The drink was cold and tart. I could feel tiny clumps of salt crystals at the corners of my upper lip and I lapped them off with my tongue. Heaven.

"Dinner," Concha sang out. She carried the hot plate with a folded towel. "You look hungry tonight, so I made three."

The three rolled enchiladas stuffed with tender chicken meat were invisible beneath the blanket of melted cheese, green chile sauce, and two dollops of sour cream. A scattering of lettuce and freshly chopped tomato covered the whole steaming platter. I could see the cheese still bubbling around the perimeter where the broiler had turned the edges crisp. Experience had taught me not to dig right in. First I cut into the side of one of the enchiladas, releasing a delicate tendril of steam. The smell made my saliva glands go into overdrive, while my eyes watered slightly from the pungency of the green chile. I finished every bite.

I had gained five pounds on my trip to Hawaii, thanks to the wonderful dinners supplied by Drake Langston. I had promised myself that I would get into some kind of exercise program when I got back but obviously I hadn't done it yet. Now this. I really would have to get serious. Maybe once I'd solved the David Ruiz case.

It was almost ten before Rusty and I got away from Pedro's. The place was dead quiet once the boisterous Manny left, so Pedro, Concha, and I sat together awhile longer, catching up. Finally, I had to let them go. I knew they must have lots of kitchen cleanup to do before calling it a night. Luckily, they don't have far to travel to get home. They live at the back of the restaurant in a little apartment they've constructed out of what probably used to be the storeroom. With their one daughter grown and gone it's just right for the two of them.

I was tempted to leave the Jeep and walk home — the exercise would have done me good. But the thought of coming back for it in the morning cooled me down. Besides, this isn't the safest neighborhood for a woman to go walking late at night. Even with Rusty at my side, I don't feel entirely at ease in the dark places between street lights.

There was a stack of mail waiting in the box, which I'd forgotten to check for two days so I stayed up awhile, drinking a cup of tea and paying a few bills. I finally hit the sack around midnight and, for some reason, was wide awake at six.

I kept thinking about Michael's comment that he thought David might be worried about money. The phone messages I'd seen on his desk from the IRS might bear that out. I felt like I needed to go back and have another look at his desk. Now that I had a direction to take, Sharon might provide some further insight as well.

The heavenly smells of fried meats, onions, and coffee greeted me when I arrived at the restaurant. Unfortunately, I still felt stuffed from the night before. I did accept a cup of coffee from Sharon as she let me into David's office once again.

The place appeared untouched since the last time I'd been there. Apparently the police had made their decision without a whole lot of checking into David's life. The messages from Tom McDonald at the IRS were still where I'd left them. I wondered if Sharon would mind if I called the man under the guise of being the accountant for the restaurant. It would be a way of finding out whether the business was involved or not. It was still early, though. Maybe I'd be better off to search through the mess in the office a bit further first.

I opened the lower desk drawer and ran my fingers through the file folders inside. One was labelled "taxes." Inside, I hit the jackpot. The restaurant had received two notices by mail of an impending audit. They were dated three months earlier. The phone calls had probably come because David had not responded to the audit notices. I was glad I'd discovered this before calling and making a fool of myself. I wondered what other little surprises the files would yield.

Specifically, I was interested in seeing the financials for the business. I found it odd that the IRS would already be auditing a business that had only existed for a year. They don't normally move that fast. Unless there was something obvious to arouse their suspicions. I rummaged through the rest of the files in the drawer but didn't come across any income statements or balance sheets. A similar search of the clutter on the desktop didn't turn them up either.

By this time, the breakfast crowd had pretty well thinned out so I took Sharon aside.

"Did David keep financial records any place besides this room?" I asked.

She looked thoughtful for a minute. "I don't think so. He did all his work here. I'm not sure I ever saw him even take anything home to do on a weekend or anything."

I thought about the apartment. There hadn't been any filing cabinets, and the small desk had contained only personal papers.

"Were you aware that the IRS had initiated an audit of the business?" I asked Sharon

Her eyes drifted toward the floor. I wasn't sure whether I just imagined the slight hesitancy.

"You mean the phone messages on his desk? I assumed that had something to do with David's personal taxes. I didn't think the business was being audited."

Something about her statement sounded weak to me. I couldn't put my finger on it but I sensed she wasn't being a hundred percent open about this. Had she and David been up to some funny business with the books?

# 11

"I need to find copies of the financials, Sharon. I've searched the desk drawer and the mess here on top. Do you have any other ideas?"

She shook her head. "What would this have to do with David's death, anyway?"

"Maybe everything." My voice came out sounding harsher than I had intended, but dammit, I hate it when people close up. "His cousin tells me that David was very nervous about something. He got the feeling it was something financial."

I held out the IRS notices and looked her straight in the eyes. "Look, I didn't know David at all, so I'm having to go by what everyone else tells me. Most people deal with life's little financial crises and somehow they cope. But some people just can't handle it. David might have felt the whole thing closing in on him and he might have seen suicide as the only way out. I know you don't want it to turn out that way but it might just be what happened."

Her facial muscles remained motionless but two large puddles formed in her lower eyelids. I waited. Sometimes silence is the best way to obligate the other person to speak.

Finally, her shoulders sagged. "I don't know about any of this, Charlie," she said, a sob escaping between the words. "David kept most of the financial aspects of this business to himself. I know I should have paid more attention but I just couldn't find the time. Charlie, you don't know what it takes to keep a restaurant going. Getting good help is the worst part. Just about the time you think you have a good crew, and everything is running all right, someone quits. You can't imagine how many times I've ended up waiting tables, or even cooking, because some little twit decided she couldn't handle the job any more and called at six o'clock that morning to let me know she wouldn't be back. So I'd do her job all day, supervise the kitchen, do the shopping, check the inventory on staples, balance the cash drawer. By the time I get home at night, I'm exhausted. In the beginning I'd take the reports home and try to study them, but I don't understand that stuff and it made my head hurt to try and make sense of them. Maybe I trusted David too far but I just couldn't do it all."

She had slumped down in David's chair and propped her elbows on the desk, her forehead in her hands. She was right —I couldn't imagine all that went into running a restaurant. I felt guilty for doubting her. Awkwardly, I patted her on the shoulder, feeling badly because I'm not one of those people who dispenses hugs and comfort easily. I let her sit there in silence a few minutes before bringing up the subject again. This time, I tried to make my voice gentle.

"For your sake, Sharon, we have to find out the state of things around here. This IRS man isn't going to give up just because no one ever returns his calls. If you'd like, I could call him, explain about David's death, and tell him we're trying to put the records together. They aren't all that cold and unfeeling. At least it will give you a little breather."

She agreed, sending a weak smile my way — the first I'd seen in awhile.

"Okay, now review with me exactly who did what. David showed you some reports. Did he produce those reports himself? Were they hand written or did he do them on the computer? Did anyone else ever review the reports — a CPA or attorney?"

Now that we were getting to some hard facts, she sat straighter in the chair and calmed down.

"David did the reports himself, on the computer. He had a CPA, Ben Murray, who did the tax returns. I think Ben reviewed the financial reports periodically, too, but I'm not sure. I couldn't stand Ben Murray. He's kind of, well, sleazy. I don't know how to describe it but I don't like being in the same room with him. I let David deal with him." She looked up at me again. "I guess I shouldn't have, huh?"

"It's okay, Sharon. What's done is done. I just need to figure out what's going on now. If David had printed reports, they have to be somewhere. I need to see them. Any ideas?"

"You could try going to see Ben Murray. I'll warn you though, wear protective bullshit gear."

We laughed, the tension broken.

I looked up Murray's address in the phone book and discovered it wouldn't be too far out of my way to stop at Dr. Casper's office first.

Linda Casper had been in my class in high school. Despite being probably the smartest of the whole bunch, she was down-to-earth. A good friend. With her head for learning and her natural bedside manner there was never any doubt she'd make a top-notch doctor. Now, just a couple of years out of med school, though, it was still a struggle. She'd gone in with two older physicians, in hopes of building her practice. It would come — just a matter of time.

When I signed the clipboard at the reception desk I noticed there were only two other patients listed for Dr. Casper. Both had already come and gone. I found myself worrying about her. Most people think becoming a doctor is an automatic ticket to riches but I knew better. I'd watched Linda sign those loan papers to get through school. It would be years before she broke even. Especially as a family practitioner, where even the best ones sometimes barely make it.

"Charlie!" Her infectious grin warmed the examining room. At five foot four, Linda is somewhat on the bosomy side, soft in all the right places for hugging a hurt child. Her short blond curls are the wash and wear variety, and her bright blue eyes go naturally with the faint freckles visible under her makeup.

"What are you in for this time?" she asked.

She consulted my folder, where her nurse had made notes about the appointment. "Removing sutures?"

She stared over the tops of her beige rimmed reading glasses. "Charlie, Charlie, Charlie," she tsked. She set the folder down, and her hands went to her ample hips. "What ever am I going to do with you?"

"Oh hush, Linda, and pull 'em out," I said with mock annoyance. I lifted my hair up, giving her a clear view.

She reached for a pair of shiny surgical scissors and some tweezers.

"What was it this time? Doesn't look like a good clean-cut knife wound." Snip, snip. I felt a small tug.

"A wrench."

"Oh, okay." Snip, snip, tug. "Are you ever going to give up these quests of yours, this insatiable need to help out the underdog?" Snip, snip.

"I doubt it."

She twisted her upper body around to look me in the eye.

"I'll bet you're working on another one right now, aren't you?"

"Well . . . "

"I knew it! I ought to suture you to this table."

"What? And take all the fun out of life?"

She laid the instruments down on the formica counter top with a little more force than necessary. I turned to see if she was really angry. Her head shook slowly back and forth, her mouth puckered into a resigned little grin.

"You haven't changed since fifth grade," she said.

I hopped off the examining table and gave her a hug. "Neither have you. Do you ever get out of here long enough to have lunch with an old friend?"

"Rarely. But it happens now and then. So, when do you want to *do lunch?*"

"I'm serious, Linda. Pick a day, and I'll be there."

"Next Wednesday. Twelve-thirty. High Noon Restaurant in Old Town."

"Watch me, I'm writing it down." I took the small spiral from my purse and made notes.

Linda scratched a couple of notes on a multiple part billing form. "Hand this to the receptionist, Charlie. There's no charge."

"Oh, no you don't," I said. I remembered that she'd only had two other patients for the day. "You can't give your services away." I looked her straight in the eye.

"Okay, minimum charge."

She gave me her *don't argue with me* look. We exchanged another hug and I left. At the front desk, the receptionist said, "That'll be twenty-one sixteen with the tax."

I gave her a check for forty and told her to adjust the billing accordingly.

Outside, the day was already turning into another warm one. A couple of cottony clouds sat atop Sandia Peak, but they didn't look quite powerful enough to build into rain producers.

Anyway, the weatherman hadn't predicted any moisture and it looked as though we might already be heading for our typical hot dry June. I let the engine idle a minute or two, then turned the air conditioner up full blast. The visit to Linda Casper had served as a pleasant interlude between investigatory duties. I proceeded toward the address Sharon had given me.

Sharon was right about Ben Murray. His office was down on South Broadway, in an area where most businesses had boarded up and left. The ones that stuck it out were heavily protected. Murray's office was upstairs over a pawn shop with windows outlined in silver burglar alarm tape, then coated with steel mesh, and finally, covered by wrought iron bars. I entered a narrow door off the street and stepped into a three foot square space facing a dilapidated wooden staircase. The closed-in area was thick with the smell of old cigarettes, with dust and mouse turds to add ambiance. Given David's inclination toward classy, expensive touches in his personal life, I had a hard time imagining him coming here for financial advice.

At the top of the steep stairs was another space about three feet square that served as landing and entrance to Murray's offices. His name had been hand lettered, probably by a six-year-old, on the opaque rippled glass panel in the top half of the door. I turned the cheap doorknob tentatively.

Murray's taste in furnishings ran to the economical. The room I stepped into was meant as a reception area. It was furnished with a wooden desk, from which various-sized chunks of the veneer were missing. An old-fashioned rotary dial phone in a peculiar shade of turquoise and an overflowing ashtray were the only visible desk accessories. A manual Royal typewriter with chipped paint stood on a metal typing stand beside the desk. It wasn't covered and had a good quarter inch of dust on it. The only other furnishings in the reception room were two matching chairs with an end table between them. They were avocado green vinyl, which coordinated beautifully with the orange and green shag carpeting — something long and treacherous, looking like it could easily harbor small rodents. Another overflowing ashtray sat on the table between the chairs.

No human being had yet taken notice of me, although I suspected tiny multi-legged creatures of the night were well aware of my presence. In the background I could hear a low monotone male voice, like one side of a phone conversation that was purposely being kept quiet. I stood awkwardly, not quite sure what to do with my hands, certain that I didn't want to sit down or touch anything. Finally, I ahummed a couple of times.

"In a minute!" The male voice became sharp and angry sounding, making me flinch. I was very tempted to tiptoe out of there, then clamber down the wooden stairs as fast as I could. Just as I began to give this serious consideration I heard the phone in the other room being returned to its cradle rather violently.

Ben Murray appeared in the doorway, almost blocking it completely. He must have been close to six-four, and at least two hundred-sixty pounds. The front two-thirds of his scalp was shiny bald, and he combed what was left straight back. The thin dishwater blond hair in back had been pulled into a rubber band, leaving a stringy pony tail about an inch and a half long. His round face showed few wrinkles and I guessed him to be about forty.

He wore a summer weight linen-looking shirt of pale yellow with no undershirt, and I could see the outline of his nipples through it. He had breasts many women would envy. He was apparently into personal decor, because he wore a heavy gold chain at his throat, a matching one, smaller, on his right wrist, a large watch with heavy gold band, a gold ring with a single turquoise nugget about the size of a nickel on one hand, and one encrusted with a similar-sized display of diamonds on the other. I was surprised to see that kind of ostentation in this neighborhood. Some of the local youth I had seen hanging around at the corner looked like they'd cut a necklace like that right off a person, just below the jugular.

Murray's cotton twill pants had formed accordion pleats on either side of the groin and at the waistband, where they crunched down to accommodate his basketball-sized belly. The buttons on the shirt were trying valiantly to keep it together across the front but it was a losing battle.

"Whatta ya want?" His voice was every bit as friendly as it had been moments earlier, making me wish I had run while I still had the chance.

"I'm here about David Ruiz," I said, sounding a lot braver than I felt.

"So?"

"Have you heard he was killed?"

"Yeah. Saw it in the paper."

"His business partner, Sharon Ortega, has hired me to check into his death." I handed him one of my business cards. "Had David mentioned the audit notices he had received from the IRS?"

His face closed, telling me nothing. "I don't have to tell you anything about my client. That's privileged information."

I wasn't sure at this point whether I wanted to let this man know that I'm a CPA myself. There is no legally privileged information between an accountant and a client. As a matter of professional courtesy, an accountant does not talk with others about his client's business, but when the law steps into it, the CPA can find himself in the slammer just as quickly as the next guy. I could see, however, with this man the only thing I'd get by arguing was a swift boot out the door.

"Look, I'm just trying to help David's partner," I said,

adopting what I hoped looked like a kindly attitude. "Sharon needs to know where things stand right now. Especially with this IRS question up in the air. I'm trying to work with her, and I can't locate any copies of the financials for the restaurant. I was hoping you might have copies in your files."

He took a step toward me and stuck an index finger at my face. "Look, Miss, you won't get anything from me. All business between David Ruiz and me was private. I got nothin' to do with him killing himself, and no file leaves this office without a subpoena attached."

"Fine. We can work it that way." I turned to the door, my hand shaking as I reached for it.

He followed me as far as the doorway but I was already halfway down the stairs. "Listen, you little bitch," he shouted, "you better not drag me into this."

I forced myself to walk slowly, as though I hadn't heard his words, but in truth I wanted to bolt. As I pulled open the outside door, I glanced back up. He was still standing at the top of the stairs, hands on hips, his lips pursed into a tight knot. I got to my Jeep as quickly as possible and locked myself safely inside. My fingers were still shaking as I fumbled the key into the ignition.

I drove several blocks before my mind settled down enough to form a plan. I realized that continuing south on Broadway would take me out to the valley. A couple of turns would get me to the Ruiz place.

The house somehow looked different, smaller and lonelier, than it had yesterday with all the cars and people around. I pulled into the driveway behind a two- or three-year-old gray Pontiac. I couldn't be sure whether it belonged to the Ruiz's or if they had company.

I was raising my hand to tap on the aluminum screen's frame when the front door suddenly opened. A little girl of about three or four stood clutching a stuffed rabbit by the ear.

She looked as startled as I felt.

"Hi," I said, smiling to put her at ease. "Are Mr. and Mrs. Ruiz at home?"

Her thumb went straight to her mouth, the rabbit dangling from her clenched fist. A woman stepped up behind her.

"Can I help you?" she asked.

"Mrs. Padilla! I'm Charlie Parker. I met you here yesterday after the funeral."

"Oh, yes, Charlie. Please, call me Esther. Come on inside." She stepped back, pushing the screen outward for me.

"I was wondering if Mr. and Mrs. Ruiz are home," I told her.

"We were just about to leave for mass," she said, looking around somewhat apologetically.

"That's all right," I assured her. "I just wanted to ask one or two questions."

"Let me find Bernice. You can visit with my granddaughter, Melissa. I was trying to keep her from going outside yet. We need to keep that pretty dress clean." She pried Melissa off her leg and gave her a gentle push toward me.

I'm always at a loss for something to say to children in situations like this. My repertoire of kiddie small-talk is sadly lacking, I'm afraid. I smiled at her and she retreated a couple of steps.

"What's your rabbit's name?" I said tentatively.

She mumbled something past her thumb and hugged the rabbit closer to her. She'd make a real protective little mommy one day.

"That's a neat vest he's wearing," I commented, thinking privately that a rabbit dressed in a pin-striped vest was an odd toy for a little girl. Usually such things were pink and fluffy, I thought. Melissa made no reply to my overtures. I was about to ask how she thought the Dow Jones would do this week when Bernice Ruiz appeared from the other room.

She was dressed in full mourning, including a black lace mantilla. Her hands fluttered a lot as she spoke and she was clearly not in much better shape than she'd been yesterday. I noticed, for the first time, that she'd brought out a lot of pictures of David. Most were eight-by-ten studio portraits in dime store gold metal frames. They began with David as an infant and went right on up to one that had to have been taken within the past year. A couple of larger frames held collages of family snapshots, and I saw a few that were probably David and his cousin Michael together at about high school age. The two boys looked remarkably alike. In a couple of the pictures, they could have easily been brothers.

I hadn't noticed that much resemblance in person, but of course I had never seen them together. I turned my attention back to Bernice.

"I'm really sorry to be bothering you so soon," I said. "I just have a question or two."

She perched primly on the edge of the afghan covered couch, indicating the ugly brown recliner for me.

"I'm trying to locate some business records that David would have had. Did he ever bring work here? Or did he keep any files here?" I knew it was a long shot, even as I asked.

She shook her head silently. Her mournful eyes didn't even look as though she truly comprehended the question.

"Did he have a special girlfriend?"

"Of course," she replied. "Libby Marquez. She's a wonderful girl from the church. So devoted to David, she was. We expected an engagement announcement any time. She sat right by my side all day yesterday." Her eyes grew bright with tears.

I had a vague memory of a girl sitting next to Bernice after the funeral. She had worn a plain dark skirt and blouse, no makeup, her hair pulled back from her face at the sides and secured with barrettes. She had held Bernice's hand, but other than that I couldn't remember much about her. From what I had seen of David, he preferred the flashy type. I remembered the photos in his office and had a hard time picturing him settling down with such a mouse.

I had one more question and I knew it would be a painful one.

"Bernice, do you know if David owned a gun?"

This time her face came alive. "No. There is no way my David would own a gun," she said adamantly.

"Are you *sure*?"

"Of course. David loved living things. Once, when he was a small boy, he threw a rock and accidentally killed a bird. That boy was heartbroken. It hurt him so badly to see that little bird die, after that he would not play with even toy guns."

"I see." A touching story, I had to admit, but people do change later in life. With David, I couldn't be sure.

# 12

I could tell she was getting restive. The others had gathered near the dining room door, waiting to leave for church.

"I'll let you get going," I said. "I wonder, though, could I take one of these pictures of David? I'll return it, of course."

Bernice seemed reluctant to part with one of the large ones, but she pulled an envelope of snapshots from the small drawer in the end table and leafed through them quickly.

"Will this one be all right?" she asked.

The photo showed David dressed in a three piece suit, standing with his arm around Sharon. They both held champagne glasses, obviously at a party somewhere. Perhaps the grand opening of the restaurant last year.

"It's fine, thanks." I said goodbye to the others, and went out to my car.

I had no definite plan where to go next so I headed back to the office. Back there, I found Sally in a slump. Her period had started, dashing her hopes of motherhood for at least another month. I spent a few minutes sounding sympathetic. The ringing telephone saved me from having to come up with something encouraging to say.

It was Sharon, checking to be sure I'd made it out of Ben Murray's office alive. I appreciated her concern. When I posed the question to her about the gun, she couldn't be sure. She had never heard David talk about a gun, but that didn't necessarily mean he didn't own one. After hanging up, I went into Ron's office and dug out the file containing the police report. The gun's serial number had checked out as being registered to David Ruiz. It had been purchased a month ago. A copy of the receipt had been found in his wallet, and photocopied for the police file. He had purchased it at A&B Coins and Guns on Central Avenue. The shop was only about three blocks from the restaurant.

I decided to stop by there later. In the meantime, I placed a call to the IRS agent who had left the messages for David. It was a good five minutes before agent Tom McDonald came on the line. He sounded young, and more harassed than hardboiled. He was interrupted twice before I got my whole story out about who I was and what I wanted.

"Now, Ms. . . . Parker, was it? I have the file in front of me. What was it you needed?"

I repeated the spiel I had just given, about how David had been killed and I was trying to straighten out his records. What I needed from McDonald was to find out what *they* needed.

"Just how far along was the audit?" I asked.

"Well, the personal audit was well underway. It's the business audit we're waiting for information on," he said.

"Personal audit?"

"That's where we noticed the inconsistencies. David Ruiz failed to provide adequate proof that his income from the partnership coincided with the level he claimed on his personal return. Additionally, his expenses triggered a red flag, forcing us to initiate an audit of the business as well."

"David was living beyond his visible means."

"Basically, yes," McDonald said.

He didn't seem terribly upset when I told him it might be several more weeks before we could put together enough information to give him what he needed. Of course penalties and interest, if owed, would continue to accrue, he reminded me. That fact established, he seemed more than happy to sit on the case for as long as it took.

This could prove to be the final setback for Sharon. Since David's estate apparently consisted of a car he'd made six payments on, a dozen five-hundred dollar suits, and his share of the business, I knew where the IRS would come looking for their money. Looked like my old friend could be in deep shit.

I didn't want to break it to her on the phone. Better to deliver the terrible news in person. To add to her troubles, the evidence was beginning to suggest that perhaps David *had* killed himself, in which case the insurance policy wasn't going to pay off. The compounding drain on her finances could well send her into bankruptcy.

Damn David! I wished he would come back to life just so I could punch him in his smug little nose. I glanced at my watch. It was already nearing five o'clock. I wasn't sure Sharon would be at the restaurant this late but I had to give it a try. Also the gun shop, like most downtown businesses, would probably be closing shortly. I grabbed my keys and purse, preparing to leave for the day.

I made it as far as the kitchen, where Ron just about opened the back door into my face.

"Hey, kid, glad I caught you," he said. He seemed in good humor. "Vicky and I are going to try out that new barbecue place tonight. Wanna come? Please . . . it's my treat."

What's got into him, I wondered. "I've got two stops to make and I need to go home to let Rusty out. Can I still make it?"

"Seven-thirty. Come by my place and we'll all ride together."

I would be cutting it close but told him I'd be there.

The street in front of Nouvelle Mexicano was deserted and, as I had suspected, the place was dark and closed up tight. I walked around the side and up the alley, which reeked from overflowing trash bins. I got no answer to my knock on the back door, either. I'd have to call Sharon at home if I got in early enough.

By the time I found the gun shop and a place to park two doors down, a middle aged man with frazzled dark hair was turning over the CLOSED sign in the window. The sign on their door said they were open till five-thirty, and my watch said it was only five-twenty. I tapped on the glass and pointed to my watch. He opened the door, although he didn't look too happy about it.

Inside, the place looked like it had been hit by a burglar with a moving van.

"Sorry, we put all the merchandise in the safe at night," he said tiredly. "If you know what you want, I could bring it out."

"I just need information," I told him, showing him my card. I pulled out the photocopy of the gun receipt. He glanced at it briefly.

"So?"

"I need to know if you remember this sale. Would you recognize the man who bought the gun?"

"What was the name again?" He looked back at the form, this time taking the time to read it. "Ruiz. Ruiz." His eyes shifted upward as he searched for a visual memory.

"He came in here about a month ago," he said, speaking

slowly like a medium in a trance. "The whole thing took about ten minutes. Guy knew exactly what he wanted. Walked in, pointed it out in the case, bought one box of ammo, signed the papers, and walked out."

"Did you check his identification?"

"He showed a driver's license. Everything looked okay to me."

"Was this the man?" I showed him the photo Bernice Ruiz had given me.

He studied it carefully. "It's hard to tell, you know? A guy at a party, smiling, had a few drinks. Looks a little different than when he's talking business, no smiles, just gets right to the point. He looked a little younger in person, too, you know. I'm pretty sure it's the same guy, though."

"And he showed his driver's license?"

"Oh, yeah. I always check that."

I thanked him and left. Something nagged at me. No one I'd spoken to had mentioned David having any knowledge of guns. In fact, his mother had pretty adamantly denied it. Yet this guy said the man walked right in and knew just what he wanted. How would David know what to buy?

I turned the Jeep around, heading west toward home. Maybe David figured a gun's a gun. Aimed point blank at your temple, probably *any* gun will accomplish the job. Assuming a knowledgeable, businesslike manner would allow him to complete the transaction with a minimum of questions. Maybe that was just David's way. Still, it bothered me.

It was seven-thirty-four when I pulled into the lot at Ron's apartment building. As usual, finding a parking spot was the real trick. Poor planning had resulted in a severe shortage of spaces. Each apartment was allotted two, which worked fine in Ron's case — one for himself and one for a visitor. However, since the majority of the tenants were young couples with two cars, their guests spilled over into any extras. Then there were the two gay guys on the second floor, whose vehicles included a twelve-year-old Mercedes, a Mustang convertible, some kind of off-road square looking thing, and a pair of matching Honda GoldWings. It always irked me that they took up so much space. If they had money for all these toys, why didn't they live in a classier place than this dump?

Visiting Ron's digs always depresses me. I hate seeing my brother live like this, when it's so unnecessary. When our parents died, they each had sizeable life insurance policies. Ron, our brother Paul, and I each ended up with about a hundred grand in cash after taxes and bills were paid. I got the family home in addition — because I was the only one still living there at the time, I guess. Our trusted family attorney managed to bilk me out of about half of mine before I wised up, but that's another story altogether. Anyway, Ron and Paul both bought homes when they married and the cash gave them a nice boost at a time most newlyweds are struggling.

About eight years ago Ron's wife, Bernadette, decided she wanted out of the marriage. She managed to take the three kids and the house and furnishings, which had all been paid for with his inheritance. Ron got his clothes and a few pieces of their old cast-off furniture. New Mexico is a community property state, but don't believe for a minute that it insures fair treatment. If one party is easy-going enough and the other party is selfish enough, anything is possible.

About that time, Ron and I decided to start the agency. I put up the money and he did most of the legwork. To this day, I have a hard time keeping a civil tongue when I have to face Bernadette. This flat-roofed brick apartment building with the paint peeling off its trim, the parking lot full of junker cars, and the perpetual noise of screaming kids is too vivid a reminder.

Ron answered his door on the first knock, jacket in hand, ready to go. I couldn't help but wonder if he didn't want me to see inside the place. He's not much of a housekeeper.

"Let's take my car," I suggested. Two boys, about seven or eight, were throwing a baseball back and forth. Neither was a very good catcher and the ball bounced off the roof of someone's old Ford while I watched.

Ron gave directions to Vicky's place, glancing nervously at his watch.

"She got another date if you don't show on time?" I teased.

"Oh, no," he said a little too brightly. "I was just checking the time."

I gave him a sidelong glance.

"Well, she made a real point of asking me to be there by seven-forty-five."

"No problem, I can step on it a little." Already I was becoming leery about the evening. I had not seen my brother quite so entwined around a female's digits since Bernadette. I really didn't want to see him start that scenario over again.

Vicky's house was just off Eubank and Academy Road, in a new subdivision jokingly called "poor Tanoan." The Tanoan Country Club is just across the road, and within its walls reside the elite of Albuquerque society. Albuquerque doesn't have a wealth of tycoons. No Gettys, Perots, or DuPonts live here. But the next best thing, the successful surgeons, lawyers, businessmen, and those who've come from California where high property values have left them searching for expensive homes, have settled into Tanoan. We're talking homes in the four- to ten-thousand square foot range. Not truly mansions, but not shabby, either. My former fiancé, Brad North and my ex-best friend Stacy, live there.

"Poor Tanoan", on the other hand, has sprung up just outside the walls for the wannabees. Lacking in sufficient status, not to mention the bucks it takes to get inside, they've settled into the grouping of impressive, albeit smaller homes on the fringes. These little places run to about three thousand square feet, and boast lots of bevelled glass front doors and landscaping that looks like it's been trimmed with nail scissors — just like the rich neighbors. Vicky's house was such a place. I felt bad about not washing the Jeep before parking it here.

"Wow, what does this girl do for a living?" I spurted out the words before I realized how it sounded.

"She's an interior designer, remember? Impressive, huh? Wait'll you see inside."

Ron pressed the doorbell. A long churchlike pealing of chimes went off somewhere far inside. Vicky opened the door almost immediately. This time she wore a pair of those stretchy black pants that look like hell on anyone over a hundred pounds. Her stomach, I noticed, was flat as a board. A stretch top that looked like it had been made out of an old pair of tights hit her just below the breasts, leaving three or four inches of well-tanned tummy showing. She started to take a step out, ready to leave immediately.

"Hey, we have a minute, don't we?" Ron said. "I wanted Charlie to see how nice you've done your place."

She glanced at her watch, making it very obvious that she didn't want to linger. Ron was unaware, though. He stepped right past her, leaving Vicky and me no alternative but to follow.

Pale shades of cream and apricot dominated the impeccable entry and living room. The latter was large enough to hold two furniture groupings, arranged to make the big room look cozier. The sofas wore an elegant cream colored silk, the side chairs were apricot velvet with a Southwestern pattern subtly woven into it. A baby grand piano in the corner had been finished in the same delicate apricot. Arrangements of silk flowers accented specific places around the room. It literally looked like a page out of *House Beautiful*. I had to admit, her taste in furnishings beat her taste in clothes all to heck.

A bookcase, floor to ceiling, filled one short section of wall. Behind its glass doors stood an assortment of all the right books, looking like they had never once been opened. A few items of personal memorabilia were arranged between them, among them a picture of a smiling baby propped up among a collection of stuffed toys. It was a nice photo, eight-by-ten in an expensive decorator frame. Somehow it looked familiar, but I couldn't imagine how.

The room's pile carpeting showed vacuum cleaner tracks, and I imagined that Vicky flinched as Ron trekked across to the far side. He pointed out the city lights view from the room's wall of glass on the west side. That was about as far as we got. Vicky hovered like a nervous mother cat, obviously eager to have us on our way. She hit a couple of light switches, plainly indicating that this was as far as the house tour would go. For an interior designer she wasn't very eager to show off her work. How did she know that I wasn't ready to do a makeover on my old place?

Vicky relaxed considerably once we reached the restaurant. We were shown to a table near windows filled with an up-close view of Sandia Peak. The booth had seats of hunter green, with a thick brass rail separating us from the next booth. A young waiter bustled about, pouring water and taking our drink orders. I searched for a topic of conversation.

"I really like your house, Vicky," I said, browsing the menu and deciding on the baby back ribs.

"Thanks," she beamed. "I did enjoy doing it." She ran her hand across Ron's lap and I got the idea she wasn't referring to her living room.

"Uh, you know, Vicky, I've been thinking about getting a new conference table for the office. What do you think, Ron? That generic work table is pretty tacky."

"Sure," he agreed, "whatever you think."

"Maybe something antique? You probably have suppliers

for that kind of thing, huh Vicky?"

"Well, uh . . . yeah sure," she agreed slowly. "I guess I could find you something." She gazed back at Ron and I'd swear she actually batted her eyes.

The food arrived then, great piles of smoky meats on platters the size of hubcaps. It was more than I'd eat at three meals, but I planned to give it a darn good try.

"Maybe later in the week," I said.

"Huh?"

"The conference table? We could go shopping later this week."

"Uh, right. Yeah." Her long fingers pulled a slice of bread apart and fed bits of it to Ron. I thought he would actually suck her fingers right there in the restaurant. I had a vivid reminder of the scene in the Ruiz kitchen.

"Were you and David Ruiz close, Vicky?" The bitch in me waited until she and Ron were about a half inch away from a lip-lock to ask the question.

Ron almost spluttered but Vicky turned to me, cool as ice.

"Not especially," she said. "Our parents have been friends for years, but David and I didn't have much in common."

"I wondered. I saw you at their house after the funeral."

She looked puzzled. "I didn't go to the funeral," she said. "My parents were there, of course. I think my sister might have been, too. I'm not sure."

What an actress. I let it drop, but I wondered what the hell she was up to.

# 13

The rabbit in the pin-striped vest. I awoke at two a.m. with one of those flashes of insight that comes from nowhere. The Padilla's granddaughter had carried that rabbit. Just like one of the stuffed toys in the photo on Vicky's bookshelf. An unusual rabbit. What was going on with that girl, and what was her connection with the Ruiz family?

After forty-five minutes of pondering the question and finding no answers, I gave up on sleep and went into the kitchen. I zapped a cup of milk in the microwave and stirred in two squirts of chocolate syrup. Rusty followed me into the living room, trying to establish eye contact, in hopes that some of the chocolate would accidentally spill into his bowl.

I picked up my novel, but couldn't get back into the story. Eventually, my eyelids started drooping and I took advantage of the moment to crawl back into bed. I had a nightmare about Ron and Vicky getting married. She wore a skin tight white dress that hit her about an inch below the buns, and we had to serve the cake off our old work table because she had refused to find an antique one for me. It was a relief when the alarm went off at seven.

Usually a hot shower will wash away the ridiculous last vestiges of a dream like that but this morning it didn't work. Perhaps because I couldn't entirely dismiss the idea as incredible. Perhaps because I still had so many questions about Vicky. Perhaps because, no matter how much the creep picked on me as a kid, I love the hell out of that shithead brother of mine.

I could feel tears mingling with the hot shower spray. I let them come. It isn't very nineties to talk this way, but sometimes a good cry really does make it all better. I stood there until the water started to run cool.

A few of Gram's blueberry muffins were still in the refrigerator and I allowed myself two. After that, I went to my closet and chose my favorite pair of pale green linen slacks and matching summer sweater. The set was a present to myself once after the breakup of a love affair. Comfort food and now comfort clothes. Rusty cocked his head to the side, definite questions in his eyes, as he watched me spritz on a shot of Giorgio. I'm sure he wondered if I were ill.

I arrived at the office before anyone else, and bopped around doing all sorts of wifely chores, making the coffee, opening the blinds, running a dust cloth over the furniture. By the time Sally arrived, I was really hitting my stride.

"Wow, you're all dressed up." She stopped in mid-step to stare. "What's the occasion?"

"Sally, just because I choose not to wear my usual jeans and T-shirt, it doesn't mean there's any *occasion*. I just like this outfit."

"Yeah, and you always wear it when something's wrong."

And I thought I'd been so cool about it.

"C'mon, what is it?" she persisted.

With anyone else, I would have commanded them immediately to butt out, but Sally knew me too well.

"It's *her*."

"I thought so," she said. "I noticed his car isn't here yet. Is
that where he is?"

"I don't know and I don't think I want to. I had dinner with
them last night and dropped them both off at his place. What
happened after that I'd really rather not envision."

I told Sally about the dream and we both had a good laugh.
Somehow telling it to someone else in the cold light of day
brought out the ludicrous side of it. I was glad I had told her.

"I'll be in my office working on payroll," I told her.

"Goody, my favorite day of the week. I'll hold all your calls."

It took hardly any time at all to enter the figures into the
computer. With just three of us, it's probably overkill to even
use computerized payroll. But it sure makes figuring the taxes
easy. The checks ran in no time and I pulled them off the
printer. I put Ron's on his desk — no sign of him yet. The file
folder on the Ruiz case was lying on his desk and I picked it
up. I carried it back to my own office after going downstairs
to hand Sally her paycheck.

Sitting at my desk, I flipped idly through the pages and
photos in the file. I was running out of threads to chase in this
case. The police had ruled suicide and so far I hadn't found
anything substantive to prove otherwise. And if it wasn't
suicide, it was murder, and I sure didn't have a clue as to who
could have done that.

Somehow, some little thing must be escaping me. I had the
feeling that once I found the little thing, the whole mystery
might just unravel at once, like chain stitching. David's death,
the IRS audit, the gun purchase, the missing financial statements, the grief-stricken relatives — all links in the chain.

One by one I flipped through the papers in the file. The

Xerox copies of the police photos were fairly good, but I had the feeling I wasn't getting certain details. One picture showed David slumped across the center console of the car. Something black, presumably blood, covered the passenger seat. There were other dark spots within the interior of the car, but in black and white I couldn't tell what they were. Seeing the original color photos might help.

I put a call in for Ron's friend in Homicide, Kent Taylor. He came to the phone after about a minute.

"Yeah, Charlie." Kent isn't too big on small talk. He's at that awkward career stage with the police force — too old to have those rookie stars in his eyes and too young to retire. He puts in his time, does a good job, and stays alive to go home at night. Safe and steady.

"Hi, Kent. How ya doing?"

"Fine." Get to the point, his tone said.

"Now that the department has closed its files on the David Ruiz case, would there be a problem with me having a look at the photos and the car? I know you let Ron have copies of the photos already. I'd just like to see the originals."

"Sure, Charlie. But the car, I'm not sure what's happened to it. It could be at the evidence yard."

"Where's that?"

He mentioned the name of a towing service that had been in business for ages. "They have the contract with the department," he told me.

"Would they let me take a look at it?"

"Not without a search warrant," he said.

Hmm. This was getting awfully complicated. I just wanted a quick peek to test my theory.

"Or, I *could* take you over there," he volunteered.

"Would you? Oh, Kent, that would be great."

"Don't get your hopes up just yet. It may have been released."

"You mean it might not still be there?"

"Well, even with a bullet hole in it, it does belong to somebody. We might have turned it over."

"Could you check, Kent? I'll come right down to look at the photos. In the meantime, if the car's still there, don't let it get away."

He agreed, but didn't seem overly concerned about it. It took me ten minutes to get to the main police station downtown, another ten to find a parking space. By the time I located Taylor, he'd pulled the file and phoned around until he ascertained that the car was indeed still at the evidence lot. When he saw how jittery I was, he laughed.

"Don't worry, kid. They won't let it go until we get there."

I prickled at the way he called me kid. He'd picked it up from Ron, no doubt. At least, thank goodness, he didn't resort to honey, babe, sweetie, or anything else sugar-coated. I don't take that kind of talk very well. But I couldn't afford to piss him off by saying anything at this point. I still needed this favor. I caught him staring at my clothes.

"Kinda dressed up, aren't you?" he commented.

"Just because you've never seen me in anything but jeans doesn't mean I don't own decent clothes."

He handed over the file and an evidence bag containing the gun without another word. Looking at pictures of dead people is bad enough when they are strangers. Although I'd only met David once, after meeting his family and hearing all about him, I felt I knew him. This all had to be mentally disconnected before I could open the file. Emotions aside, I had to look for clues, hard clues.

In full color, this was much harder to do. I forced myself not to look at David, only at the surrounding area.

"What's this?" I asked Kent, pointing to one of the photos. It was a black dot on the inside of the car door, passenger side, about a half inch below the window.

"That's where the bullet ended up," he said.

Oh. I continued to go through the photos, giving each one my full attention. Near the bottom of the stack was one taken from several feet away. It showed the car sitting in the parking lot, looking just like any other car in any other lot. This must have been how it looked to passers by, except that it was daylight in the photo. Something about the driver's side window caught my eye. There was a distinct reflection of sunlight off it.

"Kent, were all the windows of the car rolled up when the officers got there?"

He stood so he could look over my shoulder. "Sure looks that way," he said.

"Seems like it would have been really hot sitting in a parked car with all the windows up. The temperature was around ninety all last week."

Taylor shrugged. "So the guy put himself out of his misery."

I shot him a look.

"Sorry, that was a rotten thing to say." He even had the good grace to look a little embarrassed. "What are you getting at, Charlie?"

"Oh, I don't know. He left his apartment quickly, there were food wrappers on the counter. I just had the feeling he went to meet someone. If you're waiting to meet someone, you don't do it with the windows up in ninety degree heat."

"How do you know about the food wrappers?" he asked, his eyes narrowing slightly.

Uh oh. "Uh, Sharon gave me a key to his place." It wasn't really a lie. I had found the key and she had said I could try it. "Let's go take a look at that car," I said a little too quickly.

Kent apparently wasn't in the mood to dig for answers because he didn't say anything more. I took the file with me as the two of us walked outside. I decided to follow Kent in my own car so he wouldn't have to bring me back.

The Porsche was parked in an end slot, with nothing else next to it. It was like even the police didn't want the doors dinged on a car like that. From the outside, there was no sign of violent death about the car. It was shiny red, a gorgeous creature.

"What will happen to the car?" I asked.

"Well, I guess if it was paid for it belongs to Ruiz's estate. If not, then some finance company has a beautiful car with a couple of minor flaws."

The finance company wouldn't come out very good on this one. David had paid almost nothing toward the principle of the loan, so by the time they replaced the blood-soaked front seat and the door panel with the bullet hole, they'd have more in it than it was worth. Unless the company prez decided to keep it for his own, they'd probably end up moving it out through a wholesaler at a hell of a discount.

Kent opened the driver's side door for me. Immediately, I was assailed by the horrible stench of death. My stomach lurched and I motioned him to close it again. I had to take a couple of breaths of fresh air to clear my lungs. I decided I could do my investigating through the glass.

Seeing the car for real didn't tell me a whole lot more than the photos had. I tried to commit the details to memory before Kent began to get too impatient. I left the lot not knowing much more than when I got there.

# 14

I wanted to get my paycheck deposited and discovered there was a branch office of my bank nearby. I decided it would be just as convenient here as to try and catch the branch near home before closing time.

It was a perfect spring day, as only Albuquerque can have them. The sky was solid deep blue, bright enough to almost be painful to look at. Mimosa and ash trees grew out of dirt squares left periodically open in the sidewalks around the parking lot. The trees had leafed out within the past few weeks, and sparrows had already found perches in them. The sun was warm, possibly too warm if not for a tiny whiff of breeze meandering up the street.

I had filled out my deposit slip and joined the line waiting for the next available teller when I felt a small tap on my shoulder.

"Charlie?"

It was Michael Mann. He wore a dark power suit of summer wool and looked as if he'd just stepped out of the barber shop. He smelled of Aramis and money. His dark eyes held mine for several seconds. I could see why he'd managed to make a name for himself in the real estate market.

"Any more progress in David's case?" he asked.

"A few clues here and there," I said noncommittally. "Nothing I can take to the bank yet." As soon as I said it I realized where we were standing and we both had a little chuckle over it.

He glanced at the slim Piaget on his wrist. "Look," he said, "I've got to get going. I have to be in Cleveland this weekend, so I better get with it."

"Oh? Business or pleasure?" As soon as the words were out, I realized I was imitating his flirtatious manner.

"Business. This is the second weekend in a row, I'm afraid. I'd rather be with my family but my wife hates business trips, so she and our little girl are staying home." He turned to leave, reaching out once more to touch my forearm. "If anything new comes up in the case, I'd like to hear from you."

I watched his back as he walked with smooth confidence toward the door. The woman in line behind me nudged me to say it was my turn.

Ron was on the phone when I got back to the office. I could tell that the conversation concerned the cheating wife case. I really wasn't interested in hearing the details. He glanced up at me as I passed his doorway and our eyes met for a minute.

"You look nice," he mouthed, pushing the receiver aside for a second.

I wanted to throw something at him. Since when does dressing nicely for one day rate so much attention? I went across the hall to my own office. Rusty lay stretched out asleep in the corner.

"What do you think, pal? Maybe I need to class up my act

more often."

He raised his eyebrows but didn't comment.

That's when I noticed the bouquet on my desk. Anthuriums. Shades of red, from crimson to pale pink, fell in a cascade interrupted by a few touches of greenery. Hawaiian anthuriums. My heart tightened up as I reached for the card. The message made my eyes sting a little. Sally caught me holding the card to my chest and sniffing.

"He's pretty special, huh?" she said.

Embarrassed, I tossed the card on the desk and busied myself setting the flowers aside. Sally remained firmly in the doorway, one eyebrow raised. She knows me too well.

"Yeah," I admitted, "pretty special." What was I feeling here? Getting mushy all of a sudden? I grinned at her but my mouth felt tight and funny. "Now get back to work!"

She wiggled her eyebrows at me twice as she turned.

I re-read the card and stared at the flowers for a couple more minutes. Placed a call to Hawaii, although I knew he'd be at work, and left a thank-you message on his machine.

Back to business.

I stuck the Ruiz file in my lower desk drawer and began work on some correspondence that I'd been putting off. Somehow, I usually manage to get letters written more efficiently when I wait until I have lots. Pressure stimulates action, I suppose. I had finished three and started on the fourth when Ron stuck his head in my doorway.

"Busy?"

I typed two more lines to let him know that I was. "What's up, Ron?"

"Nothing much. I just wanted to let you know that Vicky and I enjoyed your company last night."

One of them probably did; the other I wasn't so sure about.

"That's quite a place she has, isn't it?" he said.

"She must be quite a successful decorator. I was hoping I'd

get to see the rest of the place. Is it just as nice as the living room?"

He looked faintly embarrassed. "Actually, I've never seen beyond the living room either," he said.

The phone across the hall in his office signalled. He ran for it, effectively ducking any further questions. My fingers lay inert on the keyboard. What a strange relationship these two had. I couldn't imagine becoming intimate with someone who wouldn't let you see beyond their living room. Vicky apparently had something to hide. I thought of the man I'd seen kissing her in the Ruiz's kitchen. Another boyfriend? A husband? And what about the dark-haired child with the stuffed rabbit? There could be any number of explanations, but my mind only gravitated toward one.

My letters finished, I was putting stamps on the envelopes by the time Ron got off the phone.

"Vicky and I are going down to the lake this weekend," he said. "You and Rusty want to come?"

New Mexico is not exactly known for its abundance of water recreation areas, and the few places we have are always jammed to the max on holiday weekends. Not my idea of fun. Half the population of Albuquerque leaves town on Memorial Day weekend, so I figure the quiet deserted city is the place to be. Besides, no matter how badly Ron wanted it, an easy friendship between Vicky and me was highly unlikely.

"No thanks," was all I said.

"We're going to get an early start, so if you change your mind before noon tomorrow, you're still welcome."

I'd rather schedule myself for dental surgery.

Sally had gone for the day, leaving outgoing mail beside her stapler. I gathered her envelopes and mine, and told Ron I'd drop them at the post office on my way out. I had decided to make one more trip across town to visit the Porsche dealer again.

The persistent blond salesman was nowhere in evidence when I arrived at the dealership, for which I was thankful. This trip required less daydreaming and more hard research. A few pieces had begun to click into place after my visit to the police garage, and I wanted to test the theory. I parked my Jeep at the side of the car showroom, hopefully out of direct line of sight of the hungry sales people's desks. Besides, it was a shady spot, where Rusty would be more comfortable while I experimented. I walked over to the car I had sat in the other day and slid into the driver's seat. The .357 Kent Taylor had showed me had about a six inch long barrel. I raised my left hand to my temple, aiming my index finger plus a few inches to approximate the length of the gun barrel. As I had suspected, with the car door closed and the window rolled up, I had to lean way to the right to make the "gun" fit. If David had leaned over as far as I did, the bullet would have ended up embedded in the passenger seat, not near the base of the passenger window, as it did. If David had tried to remain sitting upright, tucking his left elbow close to his side, the barrel would have been aimed sharply upward, causing the bullet to end up in the roof of the car.

My findings could mean only one thing: David was murdered.

# 15

I felt I should see Kent Taylor right away. He wasn't going to take kindly to the news that his department hadn't done a thorough job, but that's life. On the other hand, if I kept what I knew to myself for just a few more days, I might be able to not only come up with the how, but the who. A macho-sounding little voice inside me urged me to go for it. My good-girl little voice warned me that withholding evidence means big trouble.

"Evidence?" said the macho voice. "The police already have the evidence and they closed the case."

"You know damn well what evidence," said the sometimes dirty-mouthed good girl. "And you know damn well that they'll re-open the case when they hear about this. *And*, you know that chasing down a murderer on your own could get you damn well killed!"

Okay, okay, I agreed grudgingly, you win.

Rusty's head was hanging out the window, his tongue lolling, as I approached the Jeep. I turned the air conditioning on for him and backed out of the parking space. There was a pay phone at the gas station next door to the car dealership. I swung into their driveway to use it.

Kent Taylor was off-duty, his office informed me. No, they would not give me his home number; I could leave a message if it was urgent. I decided to use my own resources instead. It was after six, with plenty of daylight left, as I headed back across town. I was pretty sure I'd seen Kent's home number in Ron's Rolodex at the office so I made that my destination.

Rusty was happy to have the run of the back yard while I went inside to make my call. The back and sides of the property are fenced, separating us from the neighbors, and Rusty's good about hanging around without wandering off. Besides, he hadn't had his dinner yet, so I knew he'd soon be ready to go home.

I switched on a minimum number of lights as I walked through the dim offices. Ron's desk top was a mess, as usual, so I carried the Rolodex to my own. Kent's number was listed, but it took me awhile to reason out Ron's system and figure out that it would be under P for Police.

An inquisitive kid answered the phone and, after questioning what exactly I wanted, held the mouthpiece about two inches from his mouth and screamed, "Daddy!" Thankfully, I was quick with my hands, and managed to jerk the receiver away from my ear just before being deafened.

"Yyelllo." Kent's voice sounded weary. I could picture him getting up from the dinner table to take the call.

"Hi, Kent. Charlie Parker. I hope I didn't interrupt your dinner."

"That's okay, Charlie. What's up?" His words were polite, but his tone said I'd better get this over with quick.

"I've got some new findings in the Ruiz case. It wasn't a

suicide, Kent. David Ruiz was murdered."

I could hear him sigh at the other end of the line. "I'm on duty again at seven in the morning. Can it wait until then?"

"I don't know, Kent. Should it?"

The noise level in the background was steadily rising. From the shrieks and laughter, it sounded like a kindergarten in the midst of a bloody coup. I heard Kent put the receiver to his shoulder and yell at them to knock it off.

"Tonight isn't good for me, Charlie," he said. "Betty's off at some PTA meeting, and you can hear what it's like around here. I've got one in bed with the chickenpox, and the other two about to tear the walls down. No way I can get away."

"I could come up there," I volunteered tentatively.

"No, tomorrow at the station would be better," he said.

Well, I've done my civic duty, I thought as we hung up. Truthfully, I was glad he'd turned down my offer. I didn't really want to search out his house which, judging by the phone prefix, must be way up in the northeast heights somewhere. And I wasn't wild about walking into the madhouse I'd heard in the background. It had been a long day and I was ready for a glass of wine and a hot bath.

Switching off my light, I walked across the hall to Ron's office and returned his Rolodex to roughly the spot where I'd found it. The sun had set, and his room was almost black in the deepening gloom. I heard a car door slam nearby and went to the front window to check it out.

The neighborhood is one of those stuck in transition for years, composed of a combination of residences and small businesses. Except for the discrete shingle allowed next to the front doors of some, anyone driving through the neighborhood might assume it was entirely residential. It isn't unusual to hear cars coming and going near the dinner hour and I wasn't sure why I even looked now. Both Ron's office and mine face the street; a glance in that direction assured me that no one was there.

The natural light in the stairwell had dimmed to blackness by now but I knew it so well I didn't bother with lights. The polished wood handrail guided me down toward the kitchen, where I could see outlines of gray at the windows. I was feeling around in the bottom of my shoulder bag for my keys when the arms encircled me.

A grip like iron pinned my arms to my sides, while some kind of cloth was pressed over my nose and mouth. I struggled and tried to kick but the person already had the advantage of surprise. The cloth smelled sickly, and I realized it had been saturated with something — probably chloroform. I held my breath and forced my struggling to become weaker and weaker before making myself go limp. I hoped it was a rea-sonable facsimile of how a drugged person might really act. About the time I thought my lungs would burst, my attacker dropped me to the floor.

My head bounced on the hardwood floor with teeth-jarring agony. It took a few seconds for the mist to clear. I heard heavy footsteps thunder across the room. The back door crashed open against the bentwood coat rack behind it. I raised my aching head just in time to see a dark figure silhouetted against the open doorway. It vanished in less than a second.

I pulled myself up, my feet in motion well before my eyes could adjust to the swimming action before them. I stumbled down the back steps and veered to my left, assuming that the person would have headed down the driveway. A low-slung car without lights squealed on the concrete, bouncing as one back tire hopped the curb. I ran toward it but it was hopeless. The car was more than a block away by the time my wobbly legs got me to the street. I sunk down on the curb, letting my head droop between my knees, sucking air to clear my brain.

When I felt like I could stand again, I turned back toward the house. How had the man gotten inside without Rusty raising some kind of fuss? Granted, he is one of the friendliest mutts around but he wouldn't let a stranger enter the house, especially after dark, without all hell breaking loose. My eyes searched the back yard as I called to him.

That's when I began to realize that Rusty was missing.

# 16

A rush of raw adrenaline can clear your head quicker than any amount of rest. The thought that something might have happened to Rusty sent a jolt of fear through me stronger than any I'd felt while it was my own hide in danger. I reached inside the kitchen door, switching on all the lights. Floods at the corners of the building and on the carriage house lit the back yard with clarity.

I called out to him and circled the perimeter without luck. Back inside, I walked through every room and searched every closet and storeroom. Nothing. In the bathroom mirror I happened to catch a glimpse of my own face. My reddish hair had come out of its ponytail and my bangs were sticking up at odd angles. There was a smear of blood across my cheek.

My first concern right now, however, was Rusty. I re-trieved my shoulder bag from the kitchen floor, pulled out my keys, and headed for the Jeep. I rolled all the windows down, and drove slowly down the street, calling out to him as I went. There was no sign of him on our block and I felt a mounting sense of dread as I continued into the next. If my attacker had taken Rusty with him, he could be anywhere in the city by now. Tears dimmed my eyes as my mind skipped over the possibilities, including one unbidden view of the doggie morgue at the city pound. I couldn't let myself think about it.

At the intersection with Central Avenue, I pulled to the side. I didn't want to believe Rusty had gotten this far away. Something inside me held to the hope that he was still within the relatively safe confines of our quiet neighborhood. Crossing a major street meant crossing into the unlimited vastness of the city, including all those other possibilities.

I turned the Jeep around, planning to scout out all the side streets before taking that next major step. Two blocks from where I'd started, I spotted a dark form lying inert in the gutter. My heart stopped.

He was unconscious but still breathing. Bending close to his face, I caught a faint whiff of the same stuff that had been used on me. Somehow, the attacker had gotten close enough to Rusty to sedate him, although I couldn't imagine how. Given the dog's body weight, as compared to a grown person though, it probably hadn't taken much. The attacker must have put Rusty into his car. That probably explained the nearby door slam I'd heard from Ron's office. But for what purpose?

I needed to get Rusty on his feet; lifting him would have been difficult even if I wasn't still dizzy from the bump to my own head. I wondered if you can give a dog mouth-to-mouth resuscitation. I wondered if you'd want to. A notebook-sized sheet of cardboard that I found in the back seat worked pretty well as a fan and I sent as much fresh air toward his nostrils as I could. I stroked his neck and talked gently to him and gradually he began to stir. Now that I knew he was out of danger, watching him come awake was almost comical. He had a stupid look on his face like a drunk who isn't quite sure where he is. He almost landed on his face the first time he tried to jump into the Jeep. He took the second try much more cautiously, and finally dragged his back half upward with a little boost from me.

The office was still completely unlocked, I realized belatedly. I headed back there while Rusty began to snore on the back seat. In my earlier frantic search for the dog, I'd turned on every light in the building; the sight reassured me as I returned. Still, I carried my little mace canister when I went back inside. The place seemed clear. When I got to the bathroom, I noticed once again the smear of blood on my cheek.

I stepped closer to the mirror to examine it. I rinsed it off, but could not find a wound that it could have come from. It must have come off the attacker's gloves. In the kitchen I found a square of gauze on the floor where I'd fallen. It was fairly dry now, but still held the faint scent of the chloroform. I found a sandwich bag in a kitchen drawer and dropped it in. The rest of the room was pretty much unscathed. There was one smeared muddy footprint near the back door, barely visible on the wood floor. I looked at the bottoms of my own shoes. Since I had trampled right through a flower bed, it didn't surprise me to find traces of mud there. The footprint could be my own.

I knew I should probably report the attack to the police, but right now I just wanted to take my dog and go home. What could the police do anyway? The evidence was skimpy at best; a smeared footprint and a gauze square. I'd be surprised if there were any decent footprints outside. The person had run down the concrete driveway, straight to the waiting car. I couldn't give much description of the car. It had been dark and low and without lights I'd had no hope of seeing the license plate.

I knew from past experience that a call like this would be low priority. I'd probably sit around an hour or more before they even came, then be asked questions which I couldn't answer for another thirty minutes. I decided I'd just report it to Kent Taylor when I saw him in the morning.

Rechecking all the doors and windows twice, I finally locked the office and headed home. Rusty slept, sprawled out across the back seat like a lumpy fur rug. I turned the radio off and listened to his light snoring for reassurance. I hoped I'd be able to put the whole evening behind me that easily but I knew it wouldn't happen. If the attacker had intended to kill me or rob me, he'd had the perfect chance with Rusty out of the way and me supposedly unconscious. Why hadn't he? I had to believe the attack was meant as a warning.

Less than three hours ago I'd sat in the Porsche and come to the conclusion that David Ruiz's death had been murder. Two hours ago I'd reported that conclusion to Kent Taylor. Within an hour after that, I'd been jumped in my own office and my dog had been abducted. My internal antennae hummed like electric wires at the thought of someone watching my moves that closely. What else did they know? What else did they *think* I knew?

I drove past my house casually, then cruised a three block area around the neighborhood, alert for any sign of an unknown dark car. Most of the residents in my area are about Elsa Higgins' age, old enough to be my grandparents. They tuck in pretty early. Many of them don't drive at all anymore, and those who do come from an age where they learned to care for the few possessions they have. Their cars are normally parked in their meticulously organized garages at night. A car parked on the street is a rarity around here. My attacker had either decided that one scare per night is enough, or he had realized how obvious he would be coming into this neighborhood. Either way, I had soon satisfied myself that no strange cars were nearby.

Even so, I carried my flashlight and mace canister with me as I got out of the Jeep and approached my house. Rusty stayed close to me as we went inside and I did a thorough check of all doors and windows. Call me paranoid.

I microwaved water for tea, then remembered I hadn't had dinner yet. Somehow nothing sounded very good. I put Rusty's food in his bowl but he let it lie there untouched. We settled for a couple of Oreos each. I took off the slacks and sweater I'd worn all day and slipped on a lightweight summer robe. The house was too quiet. I put a couple of classical CDs into the player, keeping the volume low. It was peaceful, snuggling into the corner of my cushiony sofa with soft music and a cup of tea. Peaceful surroundings for a turbulent mind.


Kent Taylor clearly hoped I would have abandoned my quest by the next morning when I showed up at his desk at 7:05. He drew long pulls on his coffee mug, obviously forcing himself to stay polite as I began my narrative. By the time I finished, he was sitting up straight and taking notes.

"So, you think someone shot David through the open car window?" he asked.

"It had to be that way, Kent. The killer shot through the open window, then opened the door and rolled the window up." He stared at me as I took a quick breath. "I can show you. I sat in that car and pretended to point a gun at my head. David would have had to aim at a completely crazy angle, causing the bullet to end up either in the roof or the passenger seat of the car. For that bullet to go where it did, someone else had to have been behind it."

Taylor stood up and walked to his file cabinet. He pulled out his file on the case and spread the pictures out on the desk's surface.

"See?" I indicated one of the exterior shots of the car. "Imagine a line of fire from the driver's head to the inside door panel just below the window on the passenger side." I laid a pencil across the photo to illustrate my point. I knew I sounded like an eager little kid but couldn't help myself.

Kent rubbed his chin as he studied the picture. I could tell he was considering my argument but professional pride wouldn't let him admit that he hadn't figured it out first.

"There's more," I told him. "Within a couple of hours after I'd left the car lot, I was attacked in the kitchen at my office."

I dropped the plastic bag with the piece of gauze in it on his desk. He sniffed at the gauze and listened as I quickly recapped the events, including the abduction of Rusty.

"It has to be related," I told him. "The Ruiz case is the only one I'm directly involved in right now. And the only one that might send someone up for murder. It was a warning, I'm sure; if they'd wanted to kill again, they had every chance."

"I don't have enough personnel to give you protection," he warned. "Based on what you've told me, we'll reopen our investigation. You better drop back and stick with your little bookkeeper duties. Let us handle the Ruiz case."

It was all I could do to maintain my cool. I felt my "little bookkeeper" temper rising, and just managed to get out of his earshot before I began muttering loudly under my breath. By the time I reached my car, I'd graduated to all-out swearing. I knew Ron had worked hard to establish a good rapport with Taylor, but that didn't stop me from wanting to lash out at him.

Unfortunately for Taylor, he'd chosen precisely the wrong tactic to use with me. His condescension made me all the more determined to solve the case before he did. This was war.

# 17

Still fuming, I decided to visit Nouvelle Mexicano. I hoped Sharon would be free for a few minutes. It was about eight-thirty, the hour when the junior executive types were usually power-breakfasting before showing up at their offices around nine-fifteen. Sharon's share of the crowd didn't look so hot. The brief burst of business they'd enjoyed after David's death had dwindled. It was another reason I wanted to get the case solved as quickly as possible. Sharon needed that insurance money.

I walked in to find her waiting tables.

"I wish you'd been here about two hours ago," she said. We walked together toward David's office at the back. "Another of my nineteen-year-old reliables quit on me."

"I've never waited tables," I told her. "You'd probably end up having to fire me."

"Oh, I didn't mean that." She laughed as she pulled out

her keys. "I could have used your accounting expertise. I had to write a final paycheck for her and didn't know how to figure the taxes. I had to call that nasty Ben Murray. If you think he's a grouch in the middle of the day, you should hear him at six in the morning."

I didn't envy her one little bit.

"If you don't mind, I'll poke around in here a bit," I told her. "When you finish your breakfast shift, I'll fill you in on the case. There've been some interesting developments."

She looked like she wanted to ask about them right then but duty called. She tucked a stray blond lock back into its bobby-pin and headed back to the dining room.

David's office felt a little more abandoned each time I visited. The clutter had taken on a layer of dust now and an industrious spider family had claimed one corner for their own. The only change I saw was the gradually increasing stack of mail forming in the center of the desk. Bills. I had the feeling Sharon was putting them here because she wasn't sure where to turn. She'd given the impression that she didn't even know their checking account balance. She was probably afraid to write checks, not knowing whether they had any money. Maybe I ought to volunteer a little accounting time to help get things back on track.

During the night, between restless dreams and bouts of anxiety where I'd get up and check to be sure Rusty was breathing, one thing had hit me with crystal clarity. If I couldn't find David's copies of the restaurant's financial statements, I might be able to retrieve them off the computer. The more I thought about it, the dumber I felt for not having figured it out sooner. I might only be able to reprint those for the last month — I wasn't sure. Some accounting programs allow the user to keep more than one month open, others require that the previous month be closed out before it will accept any entries for the current month. At the very least, I should be able to run some kind of historical reports that would point out trends. It wouldn't be the same as having David's files, which would probably contain his notes and monthly adjustment figures, but it was better than nothing.

I spent the next hour going through every file in every drawer and every notebook and printout on the shelves. The results were no different than last time. The only thing I could figure was that David had turned everything over to Ben Murray for review. It seemed like the only logical answer, although I still had a hard time reconciling David's choice of accountants, given their very different styles.

Sharon came in just as I was switching on the computer and I told her what I intended to do. She didn't know anything about the software either but told me to go for it.

"Now I want to hear what else you've come up with," she said.

She had brought two mugs of coffee with her, so we both sat back a few minutes while I told her about my visit to the car lot and my talk with Kent Taylor this morning. I left out the part about the attack last night. The case was beginning to be an obsession with me, I knew, but I didn't want her to pull me off it because she thought it was dangerous.

"I don't know what this means as far as your insurance is concerned," I said, "but I'd think you have a much better chance of getting something out of them now that the police are investigating again."

The relief on her face was tangible. She still had difficult times ahead of her, but some cash could make all the difference.

"I'm going to leave you to your work," she said. "If you want more coffee, something to eat, hugs, kisses, anything — you just let me know."

It took me a couple of hours to work my way through their software. Luckily, David had the user's guide on the shelf and

I was able to glean enough to find out that I could reprint all the reports dating back to January. Five months worth wouldn't give me the whole picture but it was a good start. There were also some historical reports available that, while they wouldn't give a lot of detail, might help fill in the rest of the missing pieces for last year as well. I wanted to be able to look back to the time the restaurant first opened. I hoped this would do it. I explored the program's menus and was soon able to start the financial statements printing.

Their printer was ancient by computer standards, at least four or five years old, and it ran slower than Christmas. The software only allowed me to start one print job at a time, so it was pretty much a full-time babysitting chore for me. Unable to leave the room for more than a couple of minutes between pages, I used my confinement time in David's office to snoop. There wasn't much I hadn't already browsed but I did take a nice long gander at the restaurant's checkbook.

Sharon had been making deposits of the daily cash intake and with no money going out the situation didn't look too dire. However, the stack of incoming bills was quite a bit larger than it had been at the beginning of the week. I felt like I ought to run some totals and let Sharon know which ones were most urgent. On the other hand, she might resent the intrusion. I was here to find David's killer, not to give financial advice. I decided I'd casually offer to help her out. If she wanted the help, fine. If not, she could gracefully decline.

It was after noon by the time the old printer finished chattering. A stack of paper almost three inches high awaited my perusal. I could see where my weekend would be spent.

There was a tap at the door just before the knob turned and the door swung inward. Sharon was balancing a food tray on one shoulder.

"Make some space on that desk," she said, obviously needing to get rid of the tray quickly.

I swept the stacks of papers and mail to one side, and she deftly lowered the tray to the clear space. She had brought two salads, heaped high with greens and topped with sauteed strips of chicken, shreds of cheese, avocado slices, and sliced olives and tomatoes. A small dollop of sour cream decorated the center of each. Two glasses of iced tea glistened with a thin film of moisture. She had included place settings, napkins, and a small dish of after-dinner mints.

"I coerced Angeline into doing both hostess and waitress duty so I could take a few minutes to eat with you," she said.

She pulled up a chair across the desk from me and distributed the food. Dark circles showed under her eyes and a thin film of perspiration shone on her upper lip. Tendrils of hair had escaped their pins and she looked like she'd been on her feet constantly since early this morning.

"Sharon, this looks wonderful," I said. "You look like you needed the break."

"I've been here since five," she said. She took a deep breath and closed her eyes a few seconds before picking up her fork.

Neither of us said anything for about five minutes; we were thoroughly occupied attacking the food. Finally, during a breather, she eyed the stack of printouts I had run.

"Did you find what you needed?" she asked.

"Well, I've got a starting place," I told her. "I still don't know what information they contain. Thought I'd take them home over the weekend and study them."

Her eyes continued to scan the desk's messy surface. I sensed some beneath-the-surface fidgeting when she saw the stack of bills.

"Sharon, you look like you're swamped here. If there's anything I could do . . . "

"I'm not sure I could afford to pay you," she sighed. "I'll have to think about it. I should probably just make the time to get in here and do it myself."

Angeline, the young hostess, burst through the door just then. "Sharon, I need your help," she said. She was wringing her hands and bouncing slightly on the balls of her feet, obviously wanting Sharon's attention right this minute.

Sharon pushed back her chair, abandoning her half-eaten salad. If all her meals were eaten this way, I could certainly understand her thinness.

I dawdled over my own lunch, thinking she might be back any time, but it didn't happen. I still hadn't seen her by the time I picked the last lettuce leaf off my plate. There wasn't much else I could do here at the moment, so I gathered the stack of paper and my purse and left, closing David's door behind me. Sharon managed a quick wave from across the room as I headed for the front door.

At the office, Sally had left already and Ron was on the phone.

"I don't see why I can't just swing by your place and pick you up," he said. There was a pause while he listened to the corresponding explanation.

"Yeah, but I've got the car all packed and I can be out of here in ten minutes." His voice was tight.

Didn't sound like his and Vicky's weekend at the lake was getting off to a real congenial start. I passed his door without sticking my head in, anxious to unload the stack of computer printouts from my arms. I dumped them on my desk just as I heard him end the conversation.

"Okay," he said with a deep huff, "I'll wait until you can get here." He appeared in my doorway a minute later.

"Problems?"

"Sometimes I just don't understand women," he said. "We have it all planned to be out of town by noon. Now it's one thing and another."

He looked at his watch. "Almost two o'clock. And instead of having me go by and pick her up, she wants to come here.

Says something's wrong with her car so she'll have to call a cab, and now it might be another hour before she gets here."

If there's one thing I've learned in life, it's not to get involved in a lover's spat. Taking a side will *always* come back to haunt you after the lovers have made up. I pasted a sympathetic look on my face and nodded, hoping I looked sincere. He sulked back to his own office.

Vicky's story about something wrong with her car so she'd have to take a cab just didn't gel with me. Unless you are going from the airport to one of the major hotels, cabs in Albuquerque are not a practical means of transportation. They don't hang around on street corners here like they do in New York. No, that girl was hiding something. I'd bet on it. I couldn't believe Ron didn't see it, though. Even trained investigators turn blind when they fall in love, I guess.

The day's mail sat on my desk waiting to be opened. I picked up my phone and letter opener at the same time. Elsa Higgins answered on the second ring.

"Everything okay there, Gram?" I asked.

"Oh, yes, Charlie. Your little boy seems to be feeling just fine."

I've always found it ridiculous the way people talk about their pets as though they are children, but I couldn't fight it this time. After almost losing Rusty last night, I was feeling protective.

"He's out in the back yard right now," she continued.

"Outside?" A small granule of fear edged upward in my throat.

"Can you see him?" I asked.

"Oh, yes. He's at the door now, in fact. I'll let him in and give him some water."

"Good idea," I said, my voice only slightly shaky, "he's . . . used to having lots of water."

What was the matter with me, I wondered, hanging up the

phone. Gram had sounded absolutely normal, nothing appeared to be wrong. I kept thinking of the dark car. Suddenly, I wasn't too eager to be alone in the office after Ron left. I finished opening the mail and sorting it into stacks, just as I heard Vicky's cab pull up at the front.

I spied from behind my shutters as she got out and proceeded to unload enough gear for a month in the Caymans. It was only a weekend at the lake, for chrissakes. Ron, meanwhile, had clomped down the stairs and out the front door, sounding none too patient by this time. He paid the cab driver and began grabbing up Vicky's bags, carrying them to his car. I watched him cram the small trunk as full as he could get it, then toss the rest into the back seat.

Vicky stood by the curb, looking half afraid to say anything. Ron is normally such a mellow kind of guy, it was probably the first time she'd seen him get a bit testy. As he deposited the last of her junk into the back seat of his car, she approached him and turned on the charm. Even from the second story window, I could tell it was make-up time. By the time she had run one knee up and down the length of his thigh a couple of times and tickled the back of his hair with a fuchsia fingertip, I had to sit down. I wanted to be disgusted with them, but truthfully, I missed Drake. The red and pink anthuriums nodded at me from atop my bookcase.

Ron's voice drifted up the stairwell. "We're leaving now, Charlie," he shouted.

I had to clear my throat. "Okay. Go ahead and lock the front door. I'm leaving pretty soon myself." The door clicked behind him before I remembered that I should have told them to have a good time. Oh, well.

I gathered Sharon's printouts and my purse, leaving the sorted mail to be handled on Monday. Thoughts of Ron and Vicky humping away all weekend in one of those cheap little one-story strip motels down at the lake kept nagging at me.

It was more than mere horniness on my part, too. Ever since I'd met that girl, something about her would not leave me alone. I locked the back door and laid the computer papers on the passenger seat of my Jeep, as I pondered what it was about Vicky that I didn't trust. Aside from everything.

It was a little after four and I was ready to pick up my dog, take off my shoes, and have a nice cool glass of wine. But when I reached Central the Jeep turned right, heading uptown instead. It was dumb, I knew. I wasn't even sure what I hoped to find out but something was driving me toward Vicky's house.

The Friday holiday weekend traffic on I-25 north was bumper to bumper. I seriously questioned my sanity as I joined it. It took close to an hour to reach Academy Road and another fifteen minutes to make my way through the stop-and-go crush before I turned off the major street. There, at the intersection, waiting to pull out into the throng I had just left behind, sat a green Jag. Behind the wheel, Michael Mann stared straight through me, intent on watching the oncoming traffic.

Vicky's was the third house on the next block and I cruised past it once without stopping. Turning around in the cul-de-sac, I pulled to a stop in front of another equally imposing structure three doors down. Vicky's place looked inscrutable. The garage doors were down — no cars out front — sheer drapes covered all the windows. I walked up to it with a clipboard in hand, trying like hell to look like a census taker. The door chimes echoed faintly, the sound fading away into empty space. Nonchalantly, I turned my back to the door and watched the neighboring houses. Nothing moved in the hot, quiet air. The traffic on Academy made a continuous dull roaring background sound; a lone cicada chirped somewhere to my right. I walked around the side of the house, unsure what my explanation would be if I was questioned.

The back of the house was slightly less battened down than the front. Here in back, the place was three stories high. I followed concrete steps down to a wide covered patio. Uncurtained French doors led to a family room large enough to accommodate a pool table, a wet bar, and a five-part sectional sofa. The doors were securely locked.

Just beyond that another set of French doors revealed a small bedroom, too pretty to have experienced regular use. Probably a guest room. The next door I came to led into the laundry room. The glass panels in the upper half of it were freshly washed and not covered. Inside, I could see new-looking appliances — washer, dryer, and ironing table. Here, I got lucky. Some careless person, probably an unlucky housekeeper, had left the door unlocked. I twisted the knob gingerly, holding my breath and getting ready to run should an alarm go off. It didn't.

I stepped inside and closed the door softly behind me. The place was quiet as a church. The smells of furniture polish and fabric softener were prevalent. I found myself walking on tiptoe, although the place had a distinct feeling of emptiness. A narrow staircase led from the laundry room to a spacious kitchen on the main level. A bit of poking around showed me the living room and dining room I'd seen on my previous visit. Every knick-knack was precisely in place and fresh vacuum cleaner paths showed that no one had entered the living room recently. Seeing them caused me to glance around to see what kind of incriminating tracks I might be leaving, but the halls and stairs had obviously already been used, probably by Vicky and the maid, hurrying to leave for the weekend.

I kept to the already-stepped-on areas as I went upstairs. Making my way down the long hallway, I peeked into each room I came to: a guest bath with thick apricot colored towels hanging on the brass towel rack, another untouched bedroom, and a child's room. The little girl in the picture downstairs?

Each room was picture perfect and lifeless. Like the rooms in model homes, beautifully decorated but not liveable. There was almost nothing of a personal nature, until I came to the master suite and saw the wedding picture. Vicky was wearing a cloud of white veil and a form-fitted dress accented with seed pearls. The groom was Michael Mann.

# 18

They were posed gazing into each other's eyes. Vicky had the same look on her face that I'd seen directed toward my brother. I felt angry but not terribly shocked. What was she up to? I'd caught her kissing some other guy in the kitchen at the Ruiz's home after David's funeral. Now I find out she was married to David's cousin.

My hand strayed to the top dresser drawer handle. It slid open to reveal neat stacks of men's underwear and socks. *Is still married.* I pushed the drawer closed and rested my palms on the polished dresser top, closing my eyes to shut out the blurry haze swimming before me. Oh, Ron, what have you gotten yourself into this time? I wanted to cry for him. Ron might not be the prize catch of the century, but he's a good guy inside and he doesn't deserve this. Thinking about it made me want to strangle the shit out of Vicky. I had to force myself not to grab up the photograph and throw it across the room.

I backed up and sat down at the foot of the king-sized bed, trying to get my thoughts in order. Little things that had previously slipped past me began to come back. Michael had mentioned his wife to me more than once. I thought he had even said something about living in this neighborhood. I'd seen him just now, leaving on his weekend trip. Vicky had cut the timing awfully close this time. And the little girl with the rabbit, the Padilla's granddaughter —Michael's and Vicky's daughter. I rubbed my temples with the tips of my fingers. I dreaded telling Ron but how could I not? He had to know. Better from someone who cared for him than to find out accidentally. He wasn't going to believe me. I better try to find some proof. I glanced around the bedroom.

There was a feminine looking desk of white French Provincial in the corner. The top was immaculate, reminding me that my own desk at home was in need of some attention. A small framed photograph of the little dark haired girl and a bud vase with a yellow silk rose in it were the only items in sight. The drawer on the left held a small stack of bills, a checkbook, a roll of postage stamps, and several pens and pencils. I probed around all the corners, but came up with nothing of interest. The drawer on the right held a couple of flat manilla file folders, where she apparently filed the paid bills and a few other household papers. A box of feminine pink stationery sat at the back of the drawer. I pulled it out; it hadn't been opened yet. Putting the box back, I realized that the first drawer hadn't been nearly this deep.

Another look inside the first drawer told me that it had a false back. Tapping at it with my fingernail, it was easy to tell that a hidden compartment existed. I ran my fingertips around the sides and bottom of the drawer once again. A small catch was concealed underneath the drawer. When touched, it caused the drawer's false back to release. Behind the thin divider was a hidden compartment, about nine by six inches.

It contained two stacks of letters. The stationery was nothing special, plain white. The envelopes had not been mailed; in fact, were not even addressed. I lifted the top one, and slid the letter out.

Darling V.,
I'm miserable without you. Each night is torment, each day the hours drag by until I am with you. I pray that we will soon be together forever. Please, darling, find the courage to tell him that you want out. I know you don't want me to step forward yet, but I cannot wait much longer. Our times together mean everything to me. I believe you feel the same, so please act quickly. Counting the hours . . .
Your One and Only

Thankfully, the handwriting wasn't Ron's. I wasn't sure whether to laugh or cry. This pulp wouldn't even sell in a bad romance novel. Rereading the letter once again, I still wasn't sure whether to laugh or cry. It looked like Vicky was spreading herself pretty thin, so to speak. Ron would have to know about this. I flipped quickly through a few more of the letters in the stack. They were more of the same. I slipped one out of the middle of the stack, fairly certain that it wouldn't be missed. With the letters back in their spot and the false panel back in place, I doubted Vicky would know anyone had touched them. I had just closed the drawer when I heard a sound from downstairs.

My senses went on alert. I had felt impervious, with Vicky and Michael gone their separate ways for the weekend. The heavy front door closed with a firm click, then I heard the sound of heels tapping across the marble foyer. A woman's voice hummed a tune I couldn't recognize but I did realize that it was headed toward the stairs. My heart thudded as I searched for a hiding place. It was either the closet or the bathroom, and from what I could see of it, the bathroom walls were almost completely mirrored. The closet looked like my only choice. I dashed for it, hoping the door wouldn't have squeaky hinges.

The walk-in closet was almost the size of my guest room and I only had about one second to inspect it in semi-darkness before pulling the door shut, leaving myself in total blackness. The humming voice had stopped. I had no idea where my visitor had gone. Chances were, she wasn't even coming to the bedroom. Nah, chances were, the bedroom was exactly where she was coming and probably to this very closet. I tried to embed myself in a rack of hanging clothes and ended up twisting my ankle as I stumbled over shoe racks on the floor. I bit my lower lip to avoid letting loose a couple of choice words.

Who could it be? Had Vicky come back for something?

The silence was killing me. I couldn't hear footsteps on the thick plush carpet and had no idea where the woman had gone. When the humming started again, I almost jumped. She was standing at the closet door. A metallic rattle told me the doorknob was in her hand. I held my breath and tried to resemble a garment.

A murmured word or two came through, then she apparently turned away from the closet. I could hear a drawer opening, papers being shuffled. The drawer closed again. Then I remembered that I had set my clipboard down on the dresser when I spotted the wedding picture.

My stomach felt a little watery at this point and I knew it would be a matter of moments before she spotted the foreign object on the dresser. If the woman was Vicky, she would know she hadn't left it there, and my goose was about to be cooked. She would either search every inch of the house until she found me, or she'd panic and call the police to do it for her. My ears went into radar mode, trying to pick up on any little sound. A good five minutes went by without even a tiny noise.

My left foot was being pierced by the tip of a spike heel and I was in serious danger of losing my precarious balance. I had to make a move soon. I decided to risk a peek. I held my breath again as I turned the knob; it moved silently in my hand. The door came inward just enough for me to press my face to the crack. There was no one in the room.

My clipboard was still on the dresser, apparently untouched. I listened intently for another full minute before daring to leave the safety of the closet. I crossed the room to the large window which overlooked the street. The woman was just sliding into the driver's seat of a gray compact car parked at the curb. I couldn't see her face. She had long dark hair like Vicky's. The car pulled away from the house with a roar. I assumed I was alone again.

I faced the bedroom once more. What had she been doing? Was it Vicky? I walked across to the desk, clicking open the hidden compartment. The letters were gone. I looked again at the one in my hand.

Downstairs, a stack of mail had been deposited on the dining table since I'd last walked through. I glanced through it. A normal assortment, some addressed to Michael, some to Vicky. I pocketed an advertising piece with his name on it, further proof to Ron that Vicky still lived with her supposedly ex-husband.

The traffic had thinned considerably by the time I reached I-25, heading south. After making the change to I-40 at the Big I, the Jeep seemed to take on a will of its own and I found myself pulling up at Pedro's. Taking comfort in a plate of chicken enchiladas and a margarita was just what I needed. I wasn't looking forward to Sunday evening and the inevitable meeting with Ron when he returned from the lake.

# 19

My head felt thick, my eyes didn't want to open when the sun came through my window the next morning. I couldn't remember exactly how many margaritas I'd had, but it had been more than my usual one. Rusty sat at the foot of my bed, his head cocked, ears perked up.

"What're you so happy about?" I grumbled.

He wagged his way around to me, sniffing my breath. Amazingly, he didn't bolt from the room. Dogs really will stick with you through anything. I decided he was trying to tell me something about going outside. The later it got, the more urgent the request would become.

I made him wait while I went to the bathroom first and found my robe. By the time I had walked through the house to the back door, he was dancing. I opened the door for him and watched him race to his favorite corner while I measured coffee and started the brewer. While it hissed I went back and washed my face and brushed my teeth. The improvement was immediate. Five minutes under a stinging hot shower and I felt almost normal. I dug a pair of shorts out of a drawer and a new T-shirt I'd bought on Kauai. It made me think of Drake again. I tried to remember what he'd said his work schedule would be. Maybe I'd call him this weekend. By the time I had brushed my hair and pulled it back into a ponytail, I could smell the brewing coffee and realized I was hungry.

Sun poured through my kitchen window when I raised the shade. The back lawn lay like a deep green carpet. It would soon need mowing. Mother's roses, which filled the flower beds along the back and left walls were already bursting forth in clumps of color. Why did I always think of them as Mother's? They'd been *my* roses for nearly half my life now but I never saw them that way.

Rusty waited at the door. He was obviously thinking the same thing I was about breakfast. I dumped a scoop of nuggets into his bowl before I turned my attention to the fridge to see what I could come up with for myself. There was cereal, but the milk smelled a little iffy so I opted for an English muffin instead. Elsa Higgins had given me jars of jam made with the raspberries from her yard last summer. I was down to the last one. Good thing the berries would be coming back soon.

I found myself dwelling on Ron's problems and finally had to tell myself to stop it. There wasn't anything I could do about it until I could talk to him. Even then, he might not care to hear about my findings. Well, he was a grown man. Once he had the facts, he would make his own decision. In the meantime, I planned to devote myself to studying Nouvelle Mexicano's financial situation, hoping to glean something that might help Sharon out of her dilemma.

I set my plate in the sink and poured another cup of coffee. The printouts waited for me where I'd left them on the dining table. I carried the papers and my mug into my home office.

With everything spread out on the desk, I wasn't quite sure where to start. I didn't really know anything about the restaurant business but had some vague idea that they probably tried to base their profit margin on some percentage of sales, like most businesses do. I ran some percentages as a test. There didn't seem to be a lot of consistency and I found myself feeling like a swimmer against a strong current. Putting in a lot of effort but not making a lot of progress. I decided to go back to the beginning.

The first few months checked out much more consistently than recent months did. Was it because the restaurant had enjoyed such a good start, which had later tapered off, or could there be a more suspicious reason?

By this time papers covered my desk. I reshuffled them. Put everything into chronological order and brought out the calculator. My fingers raced over the ten-key pad, checking percentages, stopping at the end of each column to pencil in my results. My numbers tallied with the computer numbers. I don't know why I thought they might turn out differently but I ran them twice. I searched the pages for errors — some entry that might have been posted to the wrong account. A debit that should have been a credit. I wanted so much to find a simple mistake.

I didn't want to believe it but it was becoming obvious that David had been playing around with the books. A lot of cash passed through the place and I began to see just how easily he might have tampered with it.

The light in the room had changed. I realized it was getting late. I was amazed to see that I had worked through the whole day. It was after four o'clock. Rusty lay on the floor. He raised a sleepy head when I pushed my chair back to stretch.

"Let's get out of here for awhile," I said.

He recognized the word "out" and bounded down the hall before I pulled myself out of my chair. I grabbed his leash off the coat rack near the door and fastened it to his collar. He knew the routine. We walked toward the park four blocks away.

The temperature had cooled somewhat from earlier in the week. It felt good. In the park, the elm and sycamore trees were almost fully leafed out. A huge willow, which hung gracefully over the small pond, was already covered in soft green. A pair of ducks hit the water as soon as they sensed Rusty. He didn't even notice them. We circled the park, Rusty tugging at his leash, wanting the freedom to run. I unclipped the leash, then leaned back against a tree trunk and watched him rip off across the green. He wouldn't go far. It was his custom to act like a young pup for about three minutes, then come trailing back slowly to flop at my feet.

My mind was still full of numbers. I took several deep breaths, not really wanting to clear them away, but trying to get a fresh perspective on them. For Sharon's sake, I didn't want to find out that her partner had been embezzling. I wasn't sure how I'd tell her. I'd need more evidence before I could say for sure anyway. I thought back to the small desk in David's apartment. Had he kept bank statements? Perhaps I should get back there before the relatives had a chance to clear out the place. Monday was the last day of the month. Odds were the apartment management would expect the place to be vacated by the first.

Rusty trotted toward me, his tongue hanging impossibly far out one side of his mouth.

"Hey, boy, have a nice run?" I put my arms around his neck. His fur was hot, with that distinctive dusty doggy smell. I was suddenly glad to have him. Thursday night's attack was still too fresh for comfort. He pulled back as my hug became too confining. "Come on, kid, let's head back. We've got an errand to do."

We didn't even go into the house when we got back. I pulled

my keys from my jeans pocket and Rusty was happy to hop into the back seat of the Jeep. The sun was low over the western volcanoes by the time we arrived at David's apartment complex.

A light shone behind the living room drapes and the front door stood open. A short Hispanic man with thinning hair was just backing out.

"Excuse me," I said.

He jumped visibly and I apologized for startling him.

"The place will be available on Wednesday," he said gruffly. I peeked beyond him, noticing that David's furniture was still in place.

"I'm not looking for a place to rent," I told him. "I'm a friend of David's."

"Oh. Well, when is his stuff gonna be out? I gotta get this place rented."

"Actually, I came to organize some of it myself. I think his father is arranging to do something with the furniture."

He seemed content with that. He stepped aside. "Lock the door when you leave," he instructed.

I watched him shuffle down the sidewalk toward the center of the complex. Closing the door behind me, I once again faced the empty apartment. There were subtle differences from my last visit. The fast food wrappers had been thrown in the trash, the bathroom neatened a bit. There was fingerprint dust on quite a few surfaces. I wondered if the police had cleaned out David's desk.

They hadn't. I could tell the papers had been shuffled through, but I couldn't see that anything was missing. The bottom drawer still held a conglomeration of files and various blank notepads. Under a pad of paper headed "From the desk of David Ruiz" lay a stack of bank statements. It didn't look like the police had even noticed anything this far down.

The statements appeared to be in reverse chronological

order, like David had tossed each month's statement in on top of the last. Some of the envelopes had not even been opened. Sloppy work for a financial man.

I peeked into a couple of the envelopes that were already open. One of the statements showed a bank charge for safe deposit box rental. The key. I had completely forgotten the safe deposit box key on David's keyring. My mind churned with the possibilities. A perfect place to stash illicit cash. But if he had lots of extra cash, why would he be behind with his bills? Actually as I recalled, his personal bills, although sizeable, had been up to date. It was the restaurant, and therefore Sharon, who were suffering. Now that David was dead, it would take a court order to get into the safe deposit box. I probably should mention it to Kent Taylor, although I had the distinct feeling he was getting tired of me.

As for the bank statements, obviously I would need to take them home and compare them side by side with the business financials before I could see anything definite. I felt a little larcenous taking them with me but, after all, who would care? The police already had their chance at them. And I could return them by the time any of the family would notice.

I scanned the apartment once more but saw nothing else that would help me. I didn't have David's keyring with me, so I just twisted the lock on the inside of the doorknob and pulled it shut behind me. Rusty was sitting in the front passenger seat, nose pressed to the thin strip of open window I had left for him. It was dark now and he was worried. I bought him a cheeseburger at McDonald's to appease him.

At home, there was one message on the answering machine. Drake Langston had called to say he missed me. The sound of his voice made my throat get a little tight. He said he had to fly to the Big Island tonight and would try to call me again tomorrow.

I tossed David's bank statements on my desk next to the

restaurant printouts but was too tired to think about numbers again just yet. I dialed Sharon's number and she answered on the second ring.

"I don't know whether you're the person I should notify about this but you're the one I know the best," I began. I told her about David's landlord wanting his apartment cleared out by Monday.

"His parents are still pretty shaken up," she said. "Maybe I ought to call the cousin, Michael Mann. He lives in the same area and seems like an organized guy."

Yeah. Hearing Michael's name re-conjured all the thoughts I'd had last night about the Ron-Vicky-Michael situation. I was more than glad to let Sharon talk to him. I was not looking forward to Ron's return tomorrow evening.

# 20

Saturday night with nowhere to go and not wanting to be alone with my thoughts. My head was full of David, Sharon, Ron, Vicky, Michael, financial statements, bank statements, and mushy love letters. Frankly, I was tired of all of them.

The back of my skull was beginning to throb again. The stitches were out now but the wound was not gone. I wanted to go back in time three weeks, snuggling into Drake's arms, sipping tropical drinks in a nice restaurant beside the ocean.

I took two Tylenol, peeled off my shorts and top to slip into my snugly terry robe, and flipped open the TV schedule. Channel 14 was showing *Casablanca*. I'd probably be sorry but I turned it on anyway. Two hours later I wiped the tears off my face and felt much better. Rusty and I made a cup of hot chocolate and shared two Oreos before hitting the sack.

High, thin clouds formed a pale gray ceiling Sunday morning when I woke up. A glance at my bedside clock told me I had slept ten hours. I must have needed it. My head felt much better and I was actually eager to get back to work on Sharon's financial statements.

I pulled on an old favorite pair of sweatpants and loose T-shirt. A splash of water on my face and combing my hair back into a ponytail were my only allowances toward vanity this morning. Rusty gobbled his breakfast while I peeled an orange and made some toast. I carried this sumptuous feast into my office with me.

Almost from the start, a pattern began to emerge. David's bank account grew as the business's profits dwindled. He wasn't even smooth about it. No doubt the IRS man pegged this right away. No wonder he hadn't sounded concerned over the phone. He must have had David's number almost immediately. Poor Sharon. After the IRS attached liens for their share and David's creditors got through with the rest, it was doubtful she would retrieve much.

I wasn't looking forward to breaking the news to her. Perhaps the best way would be to make out a full report. Seeing the numbers in black and white might make it a little more real to her. I pulled out a columnar pad and began making notes. It was after one o'clock before I looked up again.

It was entirely possible that David's relatives would choose a Sunday to clear out his apartment. I began to get antsy over having his bank statements still in my possession. Maybe I ought to go by the office and photocopy them and return the originals to his place. Rusty looked eager for another outing so I grabbed the papers I needed, David's keyring, and my purse, and headed for the door.

The weather had turned decidedly cooler. The high thin clouds were now thick and dark — a rumble of low thunder sounding in the distance. I picked up a lightweight jacket, just in case.

The office had a deserted feel to it. In the two days since

anyone had been there an industrious spider had started a web across the back door. The rooms were cool and dim. I switched on lights, trying to dispel the hollow feeling. Microwaved a cup of water and made myself some tea. Rusty clicked around behind me wherever I went.

While the copier warmed up, I sorted through the papers I had brought. It would probably be a good idea to stick an extra copy of my findings into Sharon's file here, in addition to the one I planned to give her. The machine hummed as I fed the sheets into it. I didn't notice Rusty leaving the room, or see the male silhouette in my doorway until he cleared his throat.

"Ron! You big shit! You scared the hell out of me," I panted, patting my chest to get my heartbeat back to normal.

"Sorry, I didn't mean to," he said.

"So, how was your weekend?" I asked. "You're back kind of early." I was hoping like crazy that he'd say they'd fought the whole time and had broken it off. No such luck.

He practically glowed as he told me how much fun they'd had. The only reason they were back this early was because it had started raining hard, and he didn't want to be caught in the worst of the traffic in bad weather.

My mind had been so absorbed with numbers and finances that I really hadn't planned exactly how I'd bring up the subject of Vicky and Michael with him. I took the coward's way out, inviting him to dinner at six. It would give me another four hours to come up with something.

When I left, Ron was looking through the Saturday mail that had been shoved through the slot in the front door. The traffic on the freeway was not bad. The heavy clouds had moved away from the city, hovering now on top of Sandia Peak like a giant gray fur cap. I steered into a parking slot at David's apartment building about twenty minutes later.

My eyes scanned the area, wondering whether I would run

into anyone I knew but all was quiet. The apartment looked just the way I'd left it the night before. I slipped the bank statements back into their hiding place and made my way out again without being seen by anyone.

All the way home, I let myself shift back into Ron-Vicky mode, trying to plan what on earth I might say to him that evening. Maybe making his favorite dinner would help soften the blow a little. I stopped at the grocery and picked up chicken, potatoes, and fresh corn.

An hour later, I remembered why I don't cook, especially fried foods. Flour, salt, pepper, potato peels, and corn husks littered the counter tops. A fine mist of oil spatter covered my range top and probably the surrounding walls, if I looked hard enough. It would take a week to get it all off.

All I could say was, Ron better appreciate this. Kentucky Fried Chicken would have been so much easier.

By six o'clock, the kitchen was back in some semblance of order and the table was set. We would eat in the kitchen, I decided. Making his favorite dinner was one thing, but eating it in the dining room would definitely clue him in that something was wrong.

Rusty met Ron at the door and the two of them rough housed in the back yard for a few minutes while I set out the food.

"This looks great," Ron said, breathing hard from Rusty's workout.

He washed his hands, then proceeded to load his plate high with fried chicken, mashed potatoes, gravy, corn, and salad. Luckily, conversation wasn't called for right away. I commented that his face looked a little sunburned. I felt stiff and awkward and hated the fact that I was postponing what I really had to say.

"Where's the pecan pie?" Ron asked, wiping a big greasy place off his face.

I actually had one, but was wanting to save it as a peace offering. I brought it out and suggested that we brew some coffee first.

"Is it Grandma Franklin's recipe?"

"No, Elsa Higgins', actually. I wasn't *that* organized. She had it in her freezer."

"What is it, Charlie? You've been acting weird all evening. I haven't been your brother all these years without figuring out when something's bothering you."

The coffee sputtered through the drip spout, wafting mocha steam into the room, while I tried to come up with a way to begin.

"It's Vicky, isn't it?" he asked gently, pulling my chin toward him with his index finger.

I nodded.

"You think she's too young for me, don't you?" His voice was indulgent.

I shrugged. It wasn't untrue. I could sense that he was about to launch into justification of their ages, and I didn't want to get into that. He needed to know the truth.

"Ron, I think she's too *married* for you."

Denial was immediate. "She's divorced."

I reached to the top of the refrigerator where I had stashed my evidence. I handed him the envelope I had swiped from their dining room table, addressed to Michael and Vicky Mann.

"This doesn't prove anything," he protested. "It's junk mail. Incorrect names stay on those mailing lists for years."

"Ron, I was in the house. In their bedroom. His underwear is still in the dresser drawers."

"What the hell were you doing in her bedroom?" he shouted. "When were you there?"

"Friday afternoon. After you left, I decided to check things out."

"That's breaking and entering!" His face was livid.

I reached out to him but he spun away. "Ron, I went there thinking the housekeeper might still be around." It wasn't true, and he wasn't pacified. "Besides, there was an unlocked door. I might have entered, but I didn't break."

"How dare you! How dare you spy on Vicky." He shook his finger in my face, and I wanted to slap it away. He was starting to make me mad now.

"Ron, she's a cheat! She's cheating with you, and she's cheating with at least one other guy!" I was beginning to heat up, too. I reached for the other letter, the mushy love letter I'd found in her desk's hidden compartment. I shoved the letter in his face. "That is, unless you wrote this!"

He pulled the single sheet of paper from its envelope. I kept talking while he read. My voice was only somewhat calmer.

"Remember when I mentioned seeing Vicky at the Ruiz house after David's funeral? She denied that she was even there? Well, I saw her in the kitchen planting a big wet one on some guy's face. Probably the same guy who wrote this drivel. Right after she kissed him, she left. She never saw me."

Ron's body tensed like a piano wire about to break. The paper in his hand shook.

"Charlie, I just can't talk to you about this any more," he said through clenched teeth. He crumpled the letter and threw it across the kitchen. The front door slammed. A moment later I heard the Mustang's tires squeal.

It had gone worse than I ever expected.

# 21

When the phone rang, I was still standing at the kitchen sink, staring out into the blackness. It wouldn't be Ron. It would take him a couple of days to cool off enough to speak to me again. I took a deep breath and reached for the phone.

"Charlie, what's the matter?" Drake Langston's voice was low and soothing.

I didn't ask how he knew. Even though we'd had only a short time together, there was a closeness between us that I'd never had with anyone before.

"Ron just blew up at me," I told him. My voice shook as I filled him in on the soap opera situation here. As usual, he was sensible.

"Charlie, it's not your problem," he said. "Ron's a grown man and, like it or not, he's entitled to make mistakes. He'll work it out."

I knew that. Somewhere deep inside me, I'd even probably

said it to myself already.

"I just hate to see a nice guy get screwed, so to speak."

He chuckled. "Always gotta help the underdog, huh?"

I felt myself get a little defensive. What was so wrong with helping the underdog, anyway?

Again, it was as though he sensed my emotion before the words came out. He tactfully swerved the subject into a different direction.

"Mack Garvey is doing a lot better," he said. "He made a point of telling me how grateful he was to you for getting him off the hook."

Mack is Drake's friend and employer on Kauai, a nice man who got himself stretched a bit too thin and wound up being accused of murder. Another underdog.

"Anyway," Drake continued, "I guess Mack can tell that I'm pining away over here without you, so he scheduled me some vacation time next month. Would I be welcome if I showed up on your doorstep?"

I felt my heart rate pick up. "Anytime," I told him. A flash of his smile flickered through my mind and the sensuous memory of his hands made me suddenly warm.

"Don't worry about Ron, sweetheart, he'll work it out."

Ron who? Oh, yeah. "I know," I told him. "I guess I just need to back off and let him figure it out for himself."

We talked a few more minutes. Drake sounded excited about getting some time off. I promised to have both Ron's and Sharon's problems out of my way before he got here.

I cleared the plates from the table, and loaded the dishwasher. Threw the chicken bones and corn cobs into a plastic bag, knotted the top and stuffed it into the trash can under the sink where Rusty couldn't get to it. He settled for a dollop of mashed potato in his bowl. I put the unsliced pecan pie into the refrigerator and poured myself a cup of coffee.

Switching off the kitchen light, I carried my mug into the

living room and snuggled into a corner of the sofa. Rusty padded behind quietly, subdued by Ron's outburst. I scratched the dog's ears and tried to focus on Drake's call rather than the scene that had preceded it. I pressed the remote button so the TV news could work at overshadowing my problems. It droned on, only marginally effective.

Drake, here for a vacation. Sounded nice. I wondered if things between us would be the same on my turf as on his. The tropical Hawaiian nights might have accounted for much of the romance between us, after all. Well, having him here would be one way to find out.

By ten, I caught myself dozing so I shut off the TV and went to bed.

I slept badly again that night. My mind flicked back and forth, from the pleasant anticipation of Drake's visit, to the final angry words Ron had shouted at me as he left. Sharon's financial problems were close by, too. I kept phrasing and rephrasing in my head different ways to tell her about David's dishonesty. In the end, I decided perhaps the best way to do it was to lay out the pages of figures I'd written down. She, too, was a grownup. She might not like what she saw, but she'd have to deal with it. Somewhere around two a.m. I drifted off.

At six, the phone rang. Just one ring. By the time I reached for the receiver, it was obvious that it wouldn't ring again. An early morning wrong number? Or, my first thought, Ron wanting to talk again? I couldn't help but wonder how he had slept. Had he called Vicky right away or simply let himself stew about the problem all night?

With all hope for sleep gone now, I crawled from between the sheets and headed for the shower. In more ways than one, I wasn't looking forward to the office today. It could be rather tense between Ron and me. Plus, I knew I'd have to face Sharon. I'd be serving her up another set of problems, but no answers. We still didn't know who had killed David.

I pulled on jeans and a cotton sweater, deciding to postpone breakfast. It was still only seven. Rusty and I headed for the Jeep and I nosed out into the early morning rush on Central Avenue. The traffic was quite a bit lighter than it usually is at eight, so I decided to make an extra stop before going to the office.

The University Bakery was not exactly on the way, but a sudden impulse made me think that a peace offering might be in order. The best cinnamon rolls in town are made only a couple of miles farther up Central.

It's one of those places that doesn't look like much from the outside — chipped white paint, pink lettering on the sign, and a 1950s rendition of a wedding cake for a logo. But inside, the place is clean and neat. Four small tables line the walls, and the smell from the well-stocked bakery cases will just about make your knees buckle. A young couple sat at one of the tables near the windows, and a sixty-ish woman wearing a lavender skirt and pink and lavender print blouse sat picking a croissant apart at the table in the far corner.

A girl dressed in white stood behind the counter. She looked about fourteen, smiling at me with a mouth full of braces when she asked if she could help me. I ordered four cinnamon rolls. Noticing that I was keeping my eye on her, she carefully chose four nice large ones with plenty of glaze, which she placed into a white box. I dug out the correct change, wondering how I was going to keep the box out of Rusty's reach until we got to the office.

It was only when I turned toward the door that I noticed the couple near the windows. They were holding hands, having coffee and muffins. The girl was Vicky.

There was no way I could walk past silently. I approached the table.

"Hello, Vicky." Icicles dripped from my chin.

She looked up at me with a blank look. Her makeup was

much more refined today, her dark hair brushed smooth and held back from her face with two combs. She wore conservative dark slacks and a cream colored silk shirt.

"Yes?" she said formally.

"Come on, Vicky, cut it out. You can't pretend you don't know me."

Her face broke into a wide smile, her hand going to her chest. "Goodness, I guess you don't know," she laughed. It was a rich, healthy laugh. "I'm Veronica, Vicky's sister." She held her hand out to me.

"Sister? As in twins?" I felt a good two inches tall.

"Vicky never told you about having a sister, I guess," she said.

I remembered questioning Vicky about being at the Ruiz house after the funeral. She said her sister had attended, not she. Pieces were falling into place. Now that I gave him another look, the man was definitely the one I had seen in the kitchen that day.

Veronica caught my glance. "This is my fiancé, Steve Silverman."

I was feeling decidedly red in the face by now. When I looked carefully, there were slight differences in Vicky and her twin, aside from their taste in clothing. Veronica's beauty mark was at the right corner of her mouth, Vicky's had been on the left. She parted her hair in the center, while Vicky's had always been swept to one side. Veronica also had a certain maturity to her. Whether it was an impression conveyed by the clothing, or something indefinable in her face, I couldn't be sure.

"I believe I saw you in the kitchen at the Ruiz's home the day of David's funeral," I said.

"Oh? Maybe so, I left early." Did I imagine a slight blush? "Is that how you know Vicky? Through David Ruiz?"

"No, we have another mutual friend."

"Vicky and David were really close at one time. Such a shock about his death," she said.

"Yes, it was. The police said suicide, didn't they?"

"I don't think anyone close to David would believe that," Veronica said. "David's family is so religious, kind of like mine, I know they can't face the idea. Religion aside, though, I can't go for that theory either. David was a very gentle guy. I can't imagine that he'd even own a gun, much less use it on himself."

Steve spoke up. "Even if David was depressed, I'd think pills would be more his style."

"Did David have a lot of worries?" I asked. "Money, women, business problems?"

They both shook their heads. "David wasn't involved with anyone that I knew of," Veronica said. "He flirted a lot, went out with a lot of pretty ladies, but no one that he'd kill himself over."

"Maybe there was a jealous husband somewhere," I said, half jokingly.

They both smiled. "David had the kind of good looks that attracted women like magnets. But I think he had enough choices, and enough good sense, to stick with the single ones," Steve said.

"I didn't know anything about his business," Veronica said, "except that he got into that restaurant a year or so ago. We went to the grand opening for it but that was the last time I was in there."

Steve pushed his chair back. "Sorry ladies, but I have to get going." He squeezed Veronica's hand across the table.

I apologized for taking so much of their time and for the mixup. I wondered whether it had registered with Veronica that I had spoken rather coldly when I thought she was her sister. She hadn't seemed to notice.

Rusty was staring out the back window of the Jeep when I got back. I placed the fragrant box of cinnamon rolls under my briefcase beside me, and ordered him to stay in the back seat. His nose was working double time by the time I stuck the key in the ignition.

Ron's car wasn't in the parking lot when I got to the office, so Sally and I helped ourselves to first choice of the rolls. We were standing at the kitchen table and I filled her in on my amazing discovery at the bakery.

"No kidding!" Her eyes were even wider than usual. "What was she like? Another . . . "

Ron opened the back door at that moment, and Sally scooted back to her desk up front. His jeans and plaid shirt were rumpled.

"Cinnamon rolls," I told him. "It's a sorry-for-the-fight present. You can have two."

He reached for the box without comment. His face didn't look too great. The skin under his eyes sagged with new wrinkles and I got the idea that he hadn't slept at all.

"Want to talk?"

He sighed. "Sure. Let's go into your office."

He plopped himself onto my couch while I turned on the lights and set my briefcase down.

"Rough night?"

He stared at a spot somewhere in the middle of the room. "Vicky had once told me not to call her after nine o'clock at night. Said it would wake up her little girl. Last night I called around ten. A sleepy sounding man's voice answered."

"Did you talk to him?"

"I just hung up," he said.

His voice had a ragged edge to it. I wanted to go over to him and give him a hug, but we'd never been that kind of family. Now I was sorry that we weren't better huggers.

"Have you talked to Vicky about it?"

He shook his head.

"Are you going to?"

He shrugged. The conversation was about over, I could tell. Ron never had been one to share his feelings. What little I knew about his heart was the part that showed on his face. The only other time I could remember it looking this way was when Bernadette left him. It made me want to cry.

"Did you know that Vicky has a twin sister?" I asked.

"I guess there are a lot of things about Vicky I didn't know," he answered in a flat voice.

He got up from the couch, his boots scraping along the hardwood floor as he crossed the hall to his own office. I felt like such a shit for being the one who had broken the news.

My briefcase sat beside the desk. It reminded me of the second shitty thing I had to do today. Sharon wasn't going to be any happier to receive her news.

# 22

Ben Murray wore a different shirt but nothing else had changed. The gold chains and rings, the slicked back hair — he was as sleazy as ever. He sat at David's desk, looking quite territorial, when I walked in. Sharon sat across from him, acting about as assertive as a jellyfish. Whose office was this anyway?

Murray saw me standing in the doorway but didn't acknowledge me. His right index finger was stabbing at the stack of envelopes on the desk. From the little I had overheard, I gathered he was demanding payment for his services. Well, stand in line, I thought.

Each time Sharon tried to open her mouth, his finger got more adamant with the envelopes. When I saw her lower lip begin to quiver, I cleared my throat. Sharon spotted me and brightened somewhat.

"Charlie! I'm glad you're here," she said.

"Is there a problem?" I asked, letting my eyes roam slowly over the desk.

"Mr. Murray was just saying how he better take over our finances. At least until I find someone permanent."

"You didn't agree to that, did you?"

"Well . . . we were still discussing . . . "

Murray was on his feet. "This is none of your business, sweetie. Maybe you better go on and play detective somewhere else."

I could feel heat rising up my neck. I glanced again at Sharon. She was looking more helpless by the minute. Her eyes sent out strong non-verbal distress signals.

"Mr. Murray," I said, pulling myself up straighter, "I'm afraid we have no need for your services. Sharon has already made arrangements for me to handle the work. If you will please excuse us." I moved aside, indicating the door to him.

He sat back down in David's chair. "You gonna throw me out yourself?" he taunted.

Really. I'd just about had it with this jerk. If he hadn't outweighed me by more than double, it would have been tempting. I do, however, still have a few grains of good sense left in me.

"Sharon, when I arrived a few minutes ago, there was a police officer sitting in his patrol car out front. Go see if he's still there. If not, call 911 and tell them we have an intruder."

She slipped past me like a cat wanting out of the dog pound.

Murray's taunting expression didn't change but he stood up. "You're a real little toughie, aren't you, baby." His voice had all the tender qualities of a snake hissing. I was beginning to wish I hadn't bluffed about the police car outside.

Murray came around the desk. I backed out, leaving him a wide path. In the doorway to David's office he turned. His thick hand came toward me. I tried to be prepared for anything. A male voice, along with Sharon's, came toward us from the main dining room. Murray turned and flung the back door to the alley open. In less than a second, he was gone.

My knees went a little weak. Sharon came around the corner just then, followed by a young Hispanic man wearing a white apron. They stopped when they saw me standing there alone.

"He's gone," I said.

Sharon ran up to me and put her arms around me. We were both trembling.

"It's okay," I said. "I don't think he'll be back. His kind are only brave in the company of people they think they can bully."

"There wasn't any police car out there," she said, "and I called 911, but I got worried they would take too long, so I grabbed Ralph out of the kitchen, and just prayed that nasty man hadn't hurt you in the meantime."

"Slow down, slow down," I soothed. "It's all right now. Ralph, could you bring two cups of tea?"

He nodded and headed back toward the kitchen.

I guided Sharon toward the chair Murray had recently left. She clasped her hands together and stuck them between her knees to make them quit shaking. I pulled the other chair closer and faced her. Ralph came back with the tea and I handed Sharon's cup to her.

"Now, what brought him here anyway?" I asked.

"Well, he said it was because he hadn't been paid. He wanted a check today. But, Charlie, his bill only arrived on Friday."

"He was just looking for an excuse to get in here," I told her. "Did you leave him alone at all?"

"No, I was here the whole time."

"So, then he said he wanted to take over paying the bills for you, handling the restaurant's finances?"

"Yes. And on the surface, I guess that seems reasonable. I

mean, he was our CPA."

"But you don't like the man, or trust him, and you hesitated to say yes."

"That's when he really started to get hostile. Charlie, I guess I just don't do well with conflict, but I didn't know what to say next. That's when you got here." She smiled at me, finally beginning to unwind a little.

"Don't worry about it," I said. "If you'd like, I'll stay awhile and balance your checkbook. Then we can see how many of these creditors we can get out of the way. We'll pay off Ben Murray and send him a certified letter informing him that he is no longer the company's CPA. We'll demand that he relinquish all files and records pertinent to this business. Would that make you feel better?"

The relief was visible on her face.

Now for the hard part. "Sharon, before I begin painting a rosy picture for you here, there's something more you should know."

I pulled my briefcase toward me and snapped the catches open. My pages of notes lay on top. I handed them to her without comment.

"I'm not sure I understand," she said after scanning the figures quickly.

Scooting my chair around, I sat beside her and held the pages where we could both read them. "This column shows the restaurant's profit. This one shows expenses. Here are yours and David's salaries. The first few weeks you were in business, notice the profit figures. After awhile, you can see that sales dwindled slightly but expenses really jumped, leaving a much lower profit."

"That doesn't make sense. Expenses were highest in the first few weeks. They should have levelled off later."

"Exactly. And look at which expense category really jumped." I flipped through the pages until I found the breakdown. "Miscellaneous. A person who isn't being very cautious can dump anything he wants into 'miscellaneous', hoping no one will try to pin it down."

"So, you're saying that David showed a lot of miscellaneous expenses that might have been something else?"

"Sharon, I don't know an easy way to say this." I showed her the copies of David's bank statements.

She stared at them, seeing but not comprehending.

"Each month he had several deposits that correspond pretty closely with the 'miscellaneous' expenses he was showing for the business. I think David was writing himself checks."

"Stealing from our business?" Her face had gone pale, her eyes wide.

"It looks that way, Sharon." My voice came out little more than a whisper.

"But, why?" she said, more to the room at large than to me.

"David probably just got in over his head," I said gently. "He liked the fast car, the nice apartment, the expensive suits. Women were attracted to him and to his lifestyle and that made it almost impossible for him to stop."

"And those phone calls from the IRS? Had they started to figure it out?"

"I think so. David's personal return was being audited. I'm sure when they saw all this unexplained money coming into his account, they decided they better look at the business, too."

"So maybe David really did kill himself. Maybe it got to be too much for him." Large liquid pools were forming in her eyes.

"I don't think so, Sharon." I told her briefly, and without too much detail, my theory about the angle of the bullet. "Homicide Detective Kent Taylor has agreed to reopen the case. Now, we just have to figure out who would have had a reason to kill David. Perhaps someone else knew what David was doing with the books. Maybe they tried to blackmail him, he wouldn't submit, an argument broke out . . . "

"Ben Murray might be a good bet," she suggested.

"I'd thought of that. If he was on record as the company's CPA and it was discovered that dirty dealings were going on— Although I don't see Ben Murray as being quite that scrupulously honest myself. Still, I think I'll check him out a little further. It could be that he was afraid David would turn him over to the IRS as the mastermind. Murray probably has a few other little secrets he'd rather keep from the IRS as well."

"Charlie, what does this mean to me?"

"Well, you just keep running your restaurant for now. Try to keep as much money coming in as possible. I'll go over these bills and try to give you a better picture by this afternoon."

Some of her color had come back, although she still slumped in her chair. She understood that it wasn't going to be an easy mess to clean up. Even if we could get the insurance money for her, much of the settlement might have to go toward clearing up her tax obligations. But I didn't want to tell her that just yet.

I hadn't planned on spending the morning at Nouvelle Mexicano but it was turning out that way. Somehow, I just couldn't leave Sharon to face the entire mess herself. After she went back into the dining room, I sat in the swivel chair and began to sort through everything on the desk.

Aside from a few new pieces of mail, I was already fairly familiar with it. I quickly sorted everything into stacks: bills, letters, and filing — urgent and 'can wait.' The check register hadn't been balanced in almost a month but David's entries were neat and readable, so it didn't take long to get a total. Next, I totalled the bills. They were more than the cash balance so I resorted them by due dates and totalled them again. I could pay everything that was over thirty days old and pay Ben Murray in full, although Sharon wouldn't get a salary this month. I wondered if she could handle that. If not, we might have to let some of the thirty day bills slip into the sixty day category. I might have to do some rejuggling.

By two o'clock I had written the checks, Sharon had signed them, and I had filed away much of the extraneous clutter that had littered the office. I took an extra fifteen minutes to dust all the furniture and neaten up the bookshelves. The difference was remarkable. I told Sharon she would have to handle the correspondence, but seeing the organized office brightened her spirits enough that she didn't seem to mind.

She thanked me several times and had Ralph make me a chicken salad. I insisted on paying for it, telling her she needed all the cash she could get at this point. Feeling full and somewhat accomplished, I headed back to my own office.

# 23

Sally was finishing a letter when I walked in. Her shaggy blond hair had been freshly trimmed and she seemed perkier than in recent days. Flexible Sally had probably already counted her cycle days and bought another home pregnancy test kit.

Rusty had heard my car and came bounding down the stairs with such force that he almost knocked me over. After getting a pat on the head and finding that I didn't bring anything edible, the red-brown whirlwind settled at my feet.

"Ron's not here," Sally said, "but he left you a note. Wants you to set up an appointment with Lorraine Boyd to show her the pictures." She handed me a brown nine-by-twelve envelope.

The wife whose husband was cheating. I really didn't want to do it, but I guess Ron just couldn't handle that kind of thing quite yet.

"I told him we shouldn't take these kinds of cases," I told Sally.

She nodded understanding. "I guess it's your baby now."

My upper lip curled. "Anything else?"

"Nope."

Rusty followed closely as I went upstairs. My office felt warm and stuffy and smelled of sleeping dog. I opened a couple of windows. I tried to think of a way out of calling Lorraine Boyd. Maybe I could just mail the pictures to her. Decided it wouldn't be cool though, if her husband were to get the mail first.

As luck would have it, she answered on the first ring. I had only met the lady once, and tried to remember the face I was speaking to. The voice was soft and cultured, with perhaps a trace of a British accent. She suggested that we meet at four o'clock at a little coffee shop near the university.

Mail was stacked in the center of my desk. I spent the next hour opening and sorting it. I wondered what kind of woman would spend perfectly good money to have someone take pictures of her husband with a lover. Since she knew he was cheating, why not just kick him out? These were prominent people, though. Maybe she felt she'd get a better settlement if she could threaten exposure. *Maybe* she wanted to keep the jerk. Threatening to expose him publicly might make him drop the lover and become an attentive husband again. Who could say?

Ron had charged her for two days time, plus expenses. He'd had to drive to Santa Fe to catch the wayward husband going at it in a friend's condominium. All in all, I supposed it was fair compensation for what she'd gotten out of the deal.

By a quarter to four, Sally had left and Ron still wasn't back. Not much way I was going to get out of the appointment, so I gathered my stuff and my dog, closed the office, and headed for the Jeep.

The weekend rain shower had left the air feeling clean and a little cooler. Lilac scent from a house down the street filled the neighborhood. The afternoon sun on the west face of the Sandias accentuated the ruggedness of the mountain. I found myself in the mood to go home and take Rusty to the park. I'd get the meeting over with as quickly as possible, then do just that.

Driving east up Central, I found the coffee shop without difficulty. It was one of those places that had been there forever. I could remember my dad taking me there for breakfast as a kid. In college, we had gone there when we were broke because the prices were so cheap. When we weren't broke, we avoided the place because it wasn't considered cool. At four in the afternoon, only three tables were occupied. Two of them hosted groups of students, the other a lone woman. I remembered her face when I saw her.

She looked like the cliché of a woman waiting to meet a private investigator — scarf covering her hair, dark glasses. I wanted to tell her to lighten up. Suddenly I was conscious of my own attire. I didn't want her to be put off by my casual jeans and sweater. She didn't seem to notice.

She reached for the envelope, turned it toward herself, and pulled the pictures out only about two inches. Satisfied, she wrote out a check and slid it across the table to me. Only then did she speak.

"Would you care for some coffee?" she asked. Again, the soft cultured voice.

She really was very pretty. Skin like fine porcelain, maybe a little too pale. Her fingers were long and delicate, her jewelry expensive but subtle. She seemed to realize that the scarf over the hair was a bit much, especially on a warm sunny day, so she slipped it off her head. It rested casually around her neck like she had purposely arranged it that way. I could have worked thirty minutes with a scarf and not achieved that elegance.

I declined the coffee, saying I had another appointment shortly, mainly because I couldn't think what kind of conversation I could possibly make with this woman. She seemed to have a lot going for her — looks, breeding, intelligence. I couldn't imagine why she wouldn't dump a man who treated her that way and just get on with her life. I was afraid if I sat across the table from her I'd feel obligated to tell her so. Since she wasn't paying us to be candid, I figured I better go. She was still sitting at her table, staring out the window when I pulled out of the parking lot.

It was still early. I was no more than fifteen minutes from Ben Murray's office. Something had been nagging at me since the encounter with him in Sharon's office this morning. Murray must have known what David was doing with the books. I wondered, in fact, if Murray wasn't behind the embezzling scheme from the start. He could easily have been taking a percentage for himself as well, letting David have the majority of the money so he'd be sure to shoulder the blame if anyone ever caught on.

No doubt, as soon as Murray received Sharon's certified letter relieving him of his duties and asking to have all her records returned, he'd destroy anything at all that might implicate him. If she'd mailed the letter today, he'd probably receive it tomorrow. I didn't have much time.

I turned west on Central. At Broadway, graffiti decorated the walls of a boarded-up fast food place. I turned left, trying to remember how many blocks to Murray's office. The building came along quicker than I expected, on my left. The lower level pawn shop looked as secure as ever, encased in steel and mesh. No sign on the outside indicated that Murray occupied the upstairs.

Driving past the outside of the building didn't yield many clues. Obviously, I wasn't going to be able to just walk right in there and ask for what I needed. My last visit to the place was still fairly fresh in my mind. Two upstairs windows faced the street, which I guessed must be the room Murray used for his private office. The drapes were open and I didn't want to take the chance of parking across the street and having him spot me sitting there. I drove past, circled the block, and found an alley which ran behind his building. There were no windows facing the alley. The only door apparently led into the downstairs pawn shop. It had two deadbolt locks and a wrought iron grill over it. So much for the alley. I drove on through.

Two doors down from Murray's building was a small dirt lot. Four cars were parked there amid smashed beer cans, broken glass, and tumbleweeds almost the size of Volkswagens. One of the cars was a pale yellow Lincoln Towncar with a vanity plate BENNY. Ben Murray, you are so transparent.

I drove slowly past the front of the pawn shop again and noticed that they were open until six. Once they closed, I assumed that the wrought iron door would be locked, the burglar alarm set. There just didn't appear to be any way into the building after hours.

This wasn't a neighborhood where I relished the idea of sitting in my parked car on surveillance. Even with Rusty beside me, I didn't like the looks of the gang members clustered under the awning of the Circle K at the corner. I circled the block once more. I had to get into that building tonight and still hadn't a clue as to how I could do it.

It occurred to me that it might be smart to let someone know where I was. Especially if I planned a lengthy stake-out of Murray or his office. Right now, I couldn't think of any other way to get the papers I needed. Avoiding the Circle K, I decided to backtrack and look for a pay phone. In the five o'clock traffic, it wasn't easy. I had to go back up Central three blocks before I found one.

I dialed Ron's number and got the machine. I left the message that if I didn't make it home before midnight, to come looking for me, and I gave Murray's office address. I didn't realize how it might sound to Ron, thinking I was hanging around on South Broadway late at night, until I'd already hung up. Decided to call back and revise the message but I'd used my last quarter. I cruised slowly back to South Broadway.

There was a small wooden building about three doors down and across the street from Murray's. It apparently housed a dental clinic of some sort. My Jeep looked decidedly out of place next to a primer painted Monte Carlo and an Impala with the front fender gone, but there weren't many other choices. I parked and rolled all four windows down a couple of inches so Rusty and I would have some air. I kept all the doors locked and hoped no one would hassle me once they saw a large reddish dog in the car.

Thus settled, I looked back toward Murray's building. The upstairs drapes were drawn now. In the parking area, the yellow Towncar was gone. Shit! When had that happened?

My heart rate picked up. How had I missed him leaving? I was sure the Lincoln had not passed me. He must have left while I went to make my phone call. Now what? I looked at my watch. It was a little after five. He must have gone for the day. At six, that building would be sealed up like Fort Knox. Right now would probably be my only chance.

Adrenaline rushed through my veins like a drug. Rusty waited, eyes fixated on the window, as I locked him in the Jeep. I felt conspicuous crossing the street, trying to look casual yet purposeful. Feeling like a dozen eyes were upon me, I opened the street-level door next to the pawn shop. Through their inner glass door I could see a long-haired blond man behind the counter and one customer, a young girl, talking to him. Neither of them looked in my direction.

The secret to successfully doing something wrong is not to act like you're doing anything wrong. I walked purposefully up the stairs as if I were on my way to a meeting with my favorite accountant. No one accosted me.

At the top, I took a deep breath. What if Murray hadn't really gone? What if he merely enjoyed sitting in his office with the drapes drawn in the afternoons? What if his car had been stolen, not taken by him? Charlie, don't be ridiculous. Tentatively, I tried the door. It was no big surprise to find it locked. The knob, however, was every bit as chintzy as I remembered. And no deadbolt. He must have thought the armor plating downstairs was enough.

I took a thin plastic card from my purse and was inside within about ten seconds. Locked the door behind me. The air in the office almost gagged me. Cigarette butts now overflowed both ashtrays in the reception area and the entire room gave off an odor of stale smoke, grease, and sweat. I glanced into Murray's private office to assure that I was alone. The smell here was worse. The heavy fragrance of recently applied cologne mingled with the rest in a stomach churning medley. Breathing through my mouth helped some.

Since I hadn't left home this morning with any gloves in my purse, I settled for a Kleenex over my hand to help minimize any fingerprints I might leave. The drawers in the reception area yielded nothing at all of importance. After only a quick glance at them, I went into Murray's office.

The man was an unbelievable slob. Another ashtray, full to the top, sat at the edge of the desk. A file folder had gotten pushed against it, shoving the ashtray so close to the edge that breathing on it might send it to the floor. Three styrofoam cups, each about half full of cold, oily coffee occupied various positions around the desk. A Coke bottle held about an inch of brown liquid and three or four cigarette butts. About two hundred slips of paper, in miscellaneous sizes like they had been ripped from the corners of other documents, lay littered about. They were all covered with the same indecipherable handwriting.

Aside from a couple of framed certificates, the walls were bare of decoration. A plant that had died months before still hung from a macrame hanger in one corner. Probably a gift from a female, as there was nothing else in the office to suggest a concern for decor. There was a chipped black four drawer file cabinet in one corner. I made it my first target.

The drawers were not labelled so I started at the top, trying to be as quiet as possible opening and closing them. The top one held nothing of interest — a credit card imprinting machine, credit card slips in an unopened dusty cellophane wrapper, a package of pencils, a ruler, and several ledger covers with no pages inside. The second drawer held client files.

The manilla folders were bent and floppy, with the thinner ones trying to slip down between the heavy ones. I had a heck of a time trying to find labels on most of them. Once I figured out that part, I was amazed to find some well-known names among them. Ben Murray, sleaze king of Albuquerque, appeared to have some influential clients. I noted a couple of State Senators, a car dealer, and a frequently-heard-from spokesperson from the Mayor's office. Hmm . . . Now what would these important people want with Ben Murray? Almost made me want to steal the whole drawerful. Thinking about it made me remember why I was really here.

About two-thirds of the way through the drawer, I came across a file titled "Ruiz." Inside were financials from Nouvelle Mexicano. I skimmed through them briefly, just long enough to realize that Murray had been keeping a duplicate set of books for David. That was all I needed to know.

The copier on the opposite side of the room looked like an

ancient job that might make a lot of noise. I debated. I'd spent about all the time I cared to in the place. If the guy downstairs was aware that Murray had left for the day, he could very well be placing a phone call right now. If the call was to Murray, I was probably taking my life in my hands already.

I looked at the file in my hands. The minute Murray realized it was missing, he'd know exactly where to come. I pulled all the papers out of the file and set them on top of the cabinet. One of the Senator's files was pretty thick. I grabbed some of the contents, roughly the equivalent of what I'd taken, and jammed them into David's file. I stuck David's file back where I'd found it, and stuffed the stolen contents into my purse. Using my Kleenex, I closed the file drawer.

I gave the office a final glance, hoping I hadn't moved anything. The place was as disheveled as ever. Murray couldn't possibly notice that he'd had an intruder.

I used the Kleenex again to close the outer door, and turned to head down the steep stairs. The long-haired blond clerk from the pawn shop was standing at the foot of the stairs, staring up at me.

# 24

"I thought Ben had left for the day," he said. His hands were on his hips, his voice none too friendly.

Had he heard my footsteps overhead? Had he seen me close the door just now? How big a lie could I get away with?

"I guess he has," I said, rattling the locked doorknob in my hand. "I don't seem to get an answer."

His eyes were steely as I started down the stairs. With each step I tried to think what I would do next. I didn't want to have to hurt the guy. I was two steps from the bottom before his gaze wavered. Finally, he shrugged his shoulders and went back inside his own shop.

Wanting to break into an all-out run, I tried to walk away casually. I made sure I was well beyond the pawn shop windows before I crossed the street to my Jeep. It was parked far enough down the street that I didn't think he could see me unless he was standing right at the windows. I made sure he wasn't before I unlocked the door.

Rusty and I decided to treat ourselves to Pedro's enchiladas for dinner. We were early enough that Pedro had a pretty good dinner crowd. Four of the six tables were occupied, meaning that Rusty had to wait outside. Within fifteen minutes, though, two of them had left, and the remaining two were regulars, so Pedro told me to bring Rusty in. He sat quietly in his corner, minding his own business and catching tortilla chips that happened to fall his direction.

I remembered the mysterious sounding message I'd left on Ron's answering machine and decided I better clarify it. I was hoping to get the machine again, so I wouldn't have to fully explain myself but no such luck. Ron picked up on the first ring.

"Charlie, where the hell are you?" he demanded.

"At Pedro's, having enchiladas. Want to join me?"

He grumbled something about a frozen dinner in the oven. I imagined his empty apartment with the ratty furniture and the rude neighbors clumping around overhead. I felt badly for him.

"Come over for a drink later, if you like," I offered. "Meanwhile, I guess I better free up the phone here."

His goodbye came out rather mumbled and I got the idea I wouldn't be seeing him later. It was just as well. I wanted the chance to go through the papers in my purse and see if I could find a clue. There must be some link between David Ruiz and Ben Murray that would make it to Ben's advantage to get rid of David. Mere tax evasion probably wouldn't be enough. It looked like Murray had a lot bigger fish in his little pond than David Ruiz.

My enchilada plate was empty, and I still hadn't come up with any brilliant ideas. I paid my check and chit-chatted with Pedro and Concha for a couple of minutes before heading home.

The spring evening was still and warm. It was that magic time of evening when the sun has gone down but it isn't dark yet. A time of day you'd like to freeze and keep somewhere for when you need a good dose of tranquility.

I pulled my mail out of the box and let Rusty romp around the back yard while I sat on the patio and opened it. Bills and catalogs mostly.

I thought about the police and wondered whether they had any new leads on the case. Somehow, I didn't get the feeling they'd made the Ben Murray connection yet, although I couldn't be sure. What other leads were there? David's life seemed to consist of his business and his women, and having lots of nice things to impress those women. Maybe I ought to do a bit more asking around about his personal life.

Sharon had said she didn't know much about the women he dated. If she didn't know, who would? Not his parents. They seemed to believe he was serious about that girl from the church. Not likely, given the pictures I'd seen in his office of the beautiful model types he usually escorted around. A male friend might know. Tomorrow I'd do some more checking.

The light was gone and Rusty lay at my side, panting. I took him inside and gave him a scoop of his food. I had taken all the Nouvelle Mexicano financials to the office with me, so I'd have to wait until the following day to compare them with the papers I'd stolen from Murray.

When I arrived at the office the next morning, though, all thoughts of financial statements were shoved aside. Kent Taylor from Homicide was waiting for me.

"Where's Ron?" He tried to act casual, but somehow I knew it was an official visit.

"I don't know, Kent. I just got here." Wasn't that obvious? We were standing in the reception area and I turned to Sally, my eyebrows up.

She shrugged. "He hasn't checked in yet."

I steered Kent upstairs to my office. He took a place on the couch. He started to lean back but couldn't hold the pose. He ended up sitting on the edge of the cushion, his forearms resting on his knees.

"Kent, what's happened?" He was shuffling around so much, I began to worry.

"Is Ron dating a girl named Vicky Padilla-Mann?"

"Why?"

"I had a visit last night from her husband."

"You guys take philandering wives cases now?"

He shot me a get-real kind of look. The silence began to get uncomfortable.

"He didn't know she was married, Kent. He just found out, and he took it really hard. It's over now."

"Good. She's bad news. And her husband is worse."

"Michael Mann? He's a successful real estate broker. He may not be a very attentive husband but he's no Jack the Ripper, is he? He certainly provides well for her."

"You knew he was David Ruiz's cousin, didn't you?" he asked.

"Yes, in fact I first met him at the funeral."

"He told me David was messing around with some Mafia types. That he'd gotten into some money troubles with them."

"Mafia? In Albuquerque?"

"We're not talking East Coast mob families, Charlie, but yes, that kind of thing goes on here. With our drug connection to Mexico, we've managed to attract some pretty heavy hitters."

"What does this have to do with Ron and Vicky?"

"Nothing, directly. After Mann visited me last night, I decided to do some checking into his background. Found out that he had a wife named Vicky, and I remembered something

Ron had said about his girl named Vicky. I just wanted to warn him away from her. Glad to know he's already broken it off."

"Do you think Michael had some other reason for visiting you, Kent?"

This was the first clue I'd had about any drug connection, but the more I thought about the names in Murray's files, the more it made sense.

"Not that I could find out," Kent replied. "He isn't involved with the drug guys, if that's what you mean."

I debated whether to tell Kent what I knew about David's embezzling. I decided he'd been pretty candid with me and maybe I owed it to him. Not to mention that obstruction of justice charges later on could prove rather embarrassing. Briefly, I outlined for him what I'd found in going through Nouvelle Mexicano's books. I made it clear to him that Sharon had known nothing about what was going on. I left out the part about Ben Murray. He could figure out that connection for himself, if there was one. Meantime, if he rushed right over to question Murray, Ben would get suspicious and it would be pretty obvious who had been into the files last night. I wanted to have some more evidence under my belt before that little tidbit came out.

Taylor left before Ron came in, which was just as well. Ron didn't need his wounds opened again quite so soon.

I sat at my desk for quite some time, pondering everything. David involved with the mob? It could be, but somehow it just didn't fit. Everything I'd seen so far made it look like David was just a small time guy doing a little personal white collar crime. Murray might have coached him on the procedure but even with the accountant's help, he hadn't covered his tracks too well. He was nowhere near smooth enough to satisfy the mob.

And why on earth would Michael Mann go to the police with that kind of information on his own cousin? Michael and

David had been close. I remembered the pictures I'd seen at the Ruiz home. Closer than brothers.

I pulled the sheaf of stolen papers from my purse. David's file was in the cabinet in Ron's office, and I brought it to my desk. Page by page, I compared the two. Definitely two sets of books. I was surprised that David had kept the real figures in his computer at the restaurant. Murray's records showed the official set that went to the IRS, the banks, and to Sharon. David's big mistake had been in depositing so much money to his own account. When his personal return was audited, the natural place for the feds to look would be the business. No wonder he didn't want to return those phone calls.

It was after noon and Ron still hadn't come in. My stomach was telling me something, so I decided to go out for a burger. Sally said Ron had called. He had been in a meeting with the insurance company all morning in connection with his fraud case. Would probably be in around two. She was about caught up with her work and wondered if she should wait for Ron or just leave. I told her to leave. We could handle the afternoon by ourselves. I offered to bring back a burger for her but she said no. She and Ross were going shopping for new backpacks.

I was at the kitchen table, the burger and fries almost gone, when I heard Ron's car pull in. He looked about a million percent better today. At least he had shaved and his shirt was pressed.

"Thanks for delivering those pictures yesterday," he said. "I got tied up later than I thought I would."

"No problem. Hungry?" I held out the cardboard folder of french fries. He waved them away. "You doing okay?" I asked.

His gaze scooted across the floor. "Yeah. Fine."

It wasn't the time to mention Kent Taylor's visit. Ron was having enough difficulty dealing with his pain. Nothing in the David Ruiz case was relevant to him anyway. I watched him go upstairs. I crushed my hamburger wrapper, gathered the other remains of lunch, and threw it all in the trash. I couldn't stop thinking about the many facets of David Ruiz. What had happened that night in the parking lot? What had turned on him? Which of the many people in his world had wanted him dead?

The phone began ringing when I was halfway up the stairs. I dashed for it, not counting on Ron to be aware of it. I was breathless when I picked it up. It was Sharon.

"Charlie? You okay?"

I assured her I was.

"I just wanted to check on you," she said. "I got the funniest feeling last night that you might have gone back to confront Ben Murray."

"You haven't heard from him again, have you?" I asked, my stomach tightening.

"Oh, no," she assured me.

"I did go on a little fact-finding mission," I said. "But there was no confrontation."

I sensed that she wanted to hear more, but it was probably best that I keep my larcenous little escapade to myself. I told her I felt close to finding some answers and would keep her posted. I managed to end the call without giving away more than that.

I had picked up the phone while standing in front of my desk and during the conversation had walked around to my chair, stretching the phone cord as I went. Now, seated in my chair, I realized that my foot had connected with something on the floor under the desk. I reached down to pick it up. It was the letter I'd pilfered from Vicky's house. It must have fallen out of my purse earlier when I'd pulled out Murray's reports.

The paper had become somewhat dogeared. I opened it again, and reread the brief note. Suddenly, I knew who one of the key players was. To confirm it, I'd have to pay a visit.

# 25

Veronica's house was a modest one in an area of town the old timers still called "the hill." Albuquerque began in the valley near the Rio Grande river, the Old Town area. As the town spread to the east, the terrain rose. My father used to say, "I'm going up the hill." Meaning he was driving from the valley up Central to the newer area. Nowadays, of course, the city has spread in every direction, including well into the foothills of the Sandia mountains, so "the hill" really isn't so very high after all.

It was a flat-roofed square little box, probably two bedrooms and one bath, as were most of its neighbors. The yard had been landscaped in gray river rock and hardy evergreens, probably because the place was now a rental and there was less maintenance involved. Many of the neighboring homes looked more inviting with tall deciduous trees, colorful flower beds, and neatly trimmed lawns. The block hadn't gone completely over to rentals yet, as had many others in the area.

There were two cars in the driveway, a gray Honda and a five- or six-year-old Volkswagen. The kind driven by college students whose parents had a little spare money.

I rang the bell and waited. It was mid-afternoon — late enough, I hoped, that Veronica would be here. She answered after a long four minutes. She was wearing jeans and a plaid shirt, tied in a knot at the waist. Her long hair was pulled into a ponytail, and even through the screen door I could see beads of perspiration on her forehead.

"Yes?" she said, breathlessly.

"Hi, I'm Charlie Parker. Remember me? I ran into you at the University Bakery the other day?"

"Oh, yes! Goodness, what are you doing here?" She wiped her hands on the thighs of her jeans. "I'm sorry," she said, "I didn't mean to be rude. Come on in."

She held the screen open to me. "I'm just moving in," she explained. "My folks helped me move my furniture this past weekend, but I'm still putting the little stuff away. Want something to drink? I think we have some Cokes, maybe an open bottle of white wine . . . "

"No, that's all right. I didn't mean to interrupt."

"I needed a break anyway. I'm having a Coke, how about you?"

"Well, if you're getting one anyway."

I waited in the living room while she went to the kitchen. It looked like a college student's place. The furniture appeared to be the cast-offs from several parent's homes — everything at least ten years old, nothing matching. I remembered a lot of good times in friend's homes just like this.

Veronica came back with two frigid-looking red cans, the store brand, not the real thing. I pulled the top on mine, and sat in an upholstered chair that had been slipcovered with a geometric-patterned sheet. It was surprisingly comfortable.

Veronica took the sofa, planting her rear in one corner, and stretching her legs out across the cushions.

"Oh, that feels good," she said, arching her back slightly and taking a long pull on the soft drink. "I've been unpacking boxes since I got back from class at noon. I had no idea I owned so much junk."

"You have a roommate? I noticed two cars outside."

"Two, Tammy and Jennifer. Tammy's the red VW. I think she's in her room asleep. They're sisters and they share one room. I've got the other to myself. Their parents own the house but made them get a roommate to help with expenses."

She took another drink from her soda. "But that's not why you came, is it?"

"Actually, no," I said. I hadn't gone to the trouble of calling her parents on the pretense of being a school friend for this, exactly, but every tidbit of information helped. I pulled the letter out of my purse.

"Do you recognize this?"

She took it from me, her face draining of color.

"Where did you get this?"

"Where did you lose it?" I didn't think this would be the appropriate time to admit to breaking and entering her sister's house.

"I don't know," she said slowly. "With the moving and all— My parents haven't seen this, have they?"

"Not yet. Do you want to explain?"

"Steve sent me these letters. I asked Vicky to keep them for me so Mother and Dad wouldn't find them. I went over to get them from Vicky's house on Friday."

"Veronica, don't your parents know about Steve? Why would you have to hide his letters?"

She set down her drink can, and leaned back. She unconsciously stroked the letter as she talked.

"My parents are very, very Catholic. They have very, very

Catholic ideas about me someday marrying a very, very Catholic boy. Steve happens to be somewhat Jewish."

"Somewhat?"

"He's not real religious and I guess his family is just so-so about it. They aren't the problem. I guess I'm the problem. I haven't found the nerve to stand up to my parents yet."

She turned and sat up straight now, her feet on the floor. A bitter little laugh came out. "Look at me, twenty-four years old, working in a law firm — that's where I met Steve — almost through college, living at home until this week, and still under my mother's thumb."

She had the situation pretty well pegged, I thought.

"Don't worry, Veronica, you're getting there. You'll tell them when the time is right."

I drained the last of my drink and set the can on the table, giving her a few more moments to put her thoughts together.

"So, Vicky was keeping the letters for you?" I asked. "Did she ever say anything about them? Did Michael know she had them?"

"I don't think so. Vicky doesn't tell Michael everything."

Well, that was understating it a bit.

"You and Vicky seem so different," I commented. "All the twins I've ever known were so identical it was uncanny."

"We're mirror image twins," she said. "I'm right handed, she's left. I have this mole on the right side of my mouth, Vicky's is on the left. Those are the physical differences. Emotionally, though, we might not even be related at all."

She glanced around the room, like she didn't want to look directly at me. Her voice was sad when she resumed. "I don't know why we're so different. It's like Vicky has something missing inside, something like . . . I don't know . . . compassion? She doesn't seem to consider others before she acts, you know."

I knew.

"When we were little she always took whatever she wanted. She got the softer bed, the prettier dresses, the bigger cookie. My parents never seemed to notice. When we got out of high school, Vicky decided she didn't want to bother with college. She was working in a real estate office that summer and she met Michael. He was engaged at the time but she wanted him. No one was going to stop her. She set up a compromising situation where his fiancé couldn't help but catch them. Once the engagement was broken, she had him."

"Did she love him?"

"She thought she did." Veronica paused and stared again at the rug. "It's sad, but I don't think Vicky loves anyone but herself."

# 26

Veronica was still sitting on the sofa when I left. I didn't think she'd gained any truly new insights into her sister's personality during the course of our conversation, but perhaps it was the first time she'd put words to her thoughts. It must be hard to face the reality of a loved one's true nature, especially in someone as close as a twin. Especially when the picture you get is not particularly flattering.

I drove down the street a couple of blocks before stopping. I didn't want Veronica to see me sitting in my car in front of her house. Pulling the phone book from behind the seat, I shuffled the pages until I found the listing for the real estate office where Michael worked. I didn't relish the idea of facing him, particularly if the truth about Vicky and Ron had come out. Somehow, I didn't picture Vicky telling him, and I was sure Ron hadn't. He'd seen enough results of these love triangle situations to know that he'd be better off keeping his mouth shut.

The Maxwell Company had offices all over town. I tried to remember, from Michael's business card, which one he worked in. I thought it was the Uptown Plaza office. It was about twenty minutes away, so I headed that direction.

Traffic was beginning to thicken, slowing in direct proportion to people's eagerness to get home. Getting to Uptown Plaza took close to thirty minutes. Finding a parking space, at least, did not prove difficult. Obviously, the real estate crowd thinned out even earlier than most. I wondered whether Michael would still be in. The answer came when I spotted his green Jag parked at the far edge of the lot, taking two spaces, shaded by one of the few trees which dotted the parking area.

Inside, the building was almost frigid in comparison to the June heat outside. In light summer clothing, it was like walking into a refrigerator. The Maxwell Company was located on the third floor, according to the directory of white plastic letters on the wall. I pressed the up arrow next to the elevator.

William Maxwell had built his company on the wow-them-with-your-success theory. Nothing was done second rate. The real estate mega-firm was the largest in Albuquerque and they showed it. The elevator doors opened to reveal the Maxwell name and logo in thick gold lettering covering the entire wall in front of me. Carpet that felt like marshmallows and looked like the ocean on an overcast day spread out before me in a seamless expanse of blue-gray calm. Upholstered furniture of burgundy and cream stripes and patterns stood in intimate groupings, while a variety of plants and antique porcelain pieces gave the place an air of elegant homeyness. Classical music unobtrusively filled the air.

The only human in sight was a receptionist seated at an antique table, which looked to me to be of French origin. The woman was about twenty-five, dressed in a pale apricot suit with just the right number of gold jewelry accents decorating her person. She had deep chestnut hair, worn to her shoulders, in a style which managed to tread a very fine line between businesslike and sexy.

She glanced up at me but didn't speak until I approached her desk. Clearly, people in jeans were not often seen in here. The very air in the place would discourage the riff-raff.

"May I help you?" A barely disguised what-do-you-want.

I drew myself up, willing my voice to come out low and cultured.

"I'm here to see Michael Mann," I told her.

We went through a short session of b.s. about whether I had an appointment; no I didn't; she'd have to see whether he was available; what was my name. Tiresome.

I was told to take a chair. Eventually, Michael appeared from somewhere deep and mysterious, apparently surprised to see me. He faked cordiality well, though.

"Could we talk privately?" I asked, looking pointedly toward Miss Apricot Perfect.

"Certainly." He guided my elbow gently down a wide hallway.

There was more hustle going on back here than was evident from the reception area. Several of the brokers sat at their desks, their doors open. Most had their jackets off, shirt sleeves rolled up. Phone conversations tended to be lively.

The decor in the broker's offices was only slightly less formal than the reception area. Michael's door had his name in gold letters. His furniture was not antique, but it was the best you could find in a standard office furniture store. The art consisted of R.C. Gorman lithographs, signed and numbered. An eight by ten of Vicky, lips pursed, eyelids half lowered, stood on the credenza behind his desk.

He indicated the chair across the desk from himself. I let

myself sink back, adopting the most relaxed posture I could manage under the circumstances. Staring at Vicky's sexy pose irritated me, so I angled myself away from her. Now that I was here, I wasn't sure whether I wanted to discuss Vicky or David. Both problems bothered me.

Michael wasn't helping. He didn't say a word, but rested his elbow on the arm of his chair while feeding his lower lip between his teeth with his index finger. His steady brown eyes never left my face.

I'm not one who feels comfortable with long silences. If Michael knew about Ron and Vicky, he was waiting for me to broach the subject. I decided to stick to safer ground.

"How is David's family doing?"

"They'll make it."

"His mother is lucky to have good friends like the Padillas standing by her."

"Yeah."

Obviously, my visit here was unwanted and my little attempts at chit-chat weren't breaking the ice. Michael's helpful attitude the day of the funeral had vanished. I had the very uncomfortable feeling that he knew about Ron.

"The police seem to think David might have had something going with the mob," I said. "I hadn't turned up that connection myself. Did he ever say anything to you?"

"My cousin apparently had a lot of things going on that no one knew about," he said. The brown eyes had begun to bore into me.

"What do you mean?"

"Never mind. I'm sure you've turned up the important stuff."

What was he getting at? Why wouldn't he just say what he thought David had been into? He'd approached Kent Taylor with this supposed hot flash of information. Why not elaborate?

"Well, I guess this is a bad time," I said.

Obviously, he wasn't going to open up as he had before. I picked up my purse and stood up. The intercom buzzer startled me.

"Michael, your wife is on the phone," the brunette voice informed him.

"Tell her I've left for the day." His voice was sharper than expected.

My eyes strayed to the photo on the credenza.

"My wife. Vicky," he said. "A beautiful, lying, cheating little slut." The last words came out through clenched teeth.

My expression must have amused him. The corners of his mouth turned upward in a sarcastic imitation of a smile.

I felt my heart rate quicken, my breathing becoming shallow. I consciously worked at making my face neutral. I had no way of knowing how much he knew.

"Her latest fling had taken to sending letters. Sickening stuff. Very foolish, putting ones feelings in writing like that." His eyes had become hard points of obsidian. The voice was steely.

"He paid the price. Now it's her turn. Dear little Vicky is going to be out so fast she won't know what hit her." He wasn't really talking to me any more; his words were more reflection than conversation. He ran his fingers through his hair, gripping at the sides of his head as if in pain.

The office seemed too secluded now. I edged my way to the door, opening it and positioning myself for a quick break.

"I really should be going, Michael."

He gave me the oddest look, as if he weren't sure when I'd arrived. He came around the desk toward me. I was aware that the hallway and other offices had become dark and quiet. Not just quiet. Deserted.

# 27

Michael's phrases kept spinning around in my head. Somehow I had to make sense of it. I wanted to explain to him that the letters weren't Vicky's, that she'd only been keeping them for her sister. But Michael wasn't listening.

The man coming toward me didn't even resemble the composed businessman I had known as Michael Mann. His hair stuck out at wild angles where he'd run his fingers through it. His eyes were distant, as though he had somehow retreated inside himself.

"Michael," I said. My voice sounded loud and shaky to me. It echoed through the hall, and I knew the rest of the staff had gone home.

He didn't look at me. His eyes, and apparently his thoughts, were elsewhere.

I edged my way out into the hall. Walking half sideways, always keeping an eye on his door, I headed for the elevator and pressed the button. The lights were turned out now, except for a table lamp in the reception area. Dim gray light from the outside windows filtered through the open doorways of the associate's offices. Shadows, deep and eerie, filled all the corners. I could hear Michael's voice, almost chanting, the words unintelligible. The elevator wasn't coming nearly fast enough.

Michael still had not left his office when the doors behind me silently slid open. I wasn't sure I had ever been so glad to find myself alone as I was when those doors enclosed me.

My hand was shaking when I aimed my key at the door lock on my Jeep. Inside, I switched on the air conditioning so I wouldn't have to slide the windows down. A glance back toward the building revealed nothing behind its reflective windows.

Coronado shopping center was only a block away. I pulled in, looking for a pay phone. Michael's words *he paid the price* haunted me. Had he found out about Ron, and believed that Ron sent the letters? I had to find out if my brother was all right.

There were pay phones right outside Mervyn's, and I stopped in the red zone, despite the honking horn of a yellow Toyota behind me. I had thrown the change from lunch into the bottom of my purse; now I pawed through the top layers of junk looking for a quarter.

I dialed the number for our second line, our after-hours code that it was one of us calling. Ron answered on the third ring.

"Ron, thank God!" Religion comes to me only under duress.

"What's the matter, Charlie?"

It took a minute for my breathing to slow down enough to talk coherently.

"Is everything okay, Ron? Are you alone?"

"Yeah . . . Charlie, *what* is wrong?"

I knew I sounded completely overwrought and was beginning to feel a little foolish.

"Nothing, I guess. I just . . . well, I'll tell you later. I'm on my way there. Will you be around?"

"For another hour or so, I guess," he said. "You sure everything's okay?"

"Yeah, fine." I took a deep breath of warm summer air. Out here in the late afternoon sunshine, my experience in Michael's office seemed like a weird dream.

I hung up the phone and got back in my Jeep, just about the time I noticed a shopping center security patrol eyeing it. I was out of the red zone and moving toward the exit before he had a chance to say anything.

The shortest way back to the office would be to take I-40 all the way to Twelfth Street, but at this time of day, it wouldn't necessarily be the quickest. I debated the options a moment too long, and missed the on-ramp. Now it would have to be either Lomas or Central. I opted for Lomas after making a last-second lane change. It was after this foolishly quick maneuver that I thought I spotted a green Jaguar behind me.

Traffic was too heavy for me to keep looking at my rearview mirror. I slowed down, letting a number of cars pass me, and infuriating those directly behind me who had no hope of changing lanes. A couple of times I thought I glimpsed that distinctive dark green again, but I couldn't be sure. If he was back there it was no accident. He was purposely staying far enough behind that I couldn't know for sure.

At San Mateo I decided to change course. I turned south, and one block later made a quick left. By the time I circled the block and emerged again on Lomas I was behind the group of traffic I'd been a part of. My eyes scanned the cars ahead of me, but no sight of a Jaguar. I was certain he hadn't followed my little detour but where was he? I sped up, weaving my way through the group. No green car. Perhaps I'd been mistaken all along.

For the rest of the trip, though, I couldn't help being on alert. Ahead, behind, around me — no green car appeared.

By the time I reached the office I was feeling somewhat foolish, like a skittish old lady seeing ghosts. I decided not to tell Ron what a baby I'd been. His car was in its regular spot out back, and I parked beside it.

The knob to the back door turned easily in my hand. Ron, as usual, had left it unlocked. How many times had I told him that it wasn't smart to be there alone after hours without locking the door.

"Ron!"

"In my office." His voice drifted down the stairs faintly.

Rusty was a little more enthusiastic to see me. At the sound of my voice he came bounding down. Amazingly, he didn't trip over himself on the stairs.

"Hey, boy." I rubbed his ears and he smiled up at me.

I walked toward Ron's office, Rusty close at my heels. Ron was at his desk, files spread out in front of him when I poked my head in.

"Everything going okay?" I asked.

"Just finishing up the paperwork on that insurance case," he said. He looked up at me, his eyes narrowing slightly. "What was that phone call all about?" he asked.

I debated how much to tell him. I didn't want to sound like the huge chicken I was beginning to feel like. But, then again, it really wasn't fair to keep him in the dark. Painful as it might be, his involvement with Vicky was trouble. Whether Michael actually knew Ron was the other man yet, I couldn't be sure. But I was sure he planned to confront Vicky, and if, in a fit of confession, she named names, Ron had the right to know he might be in danger.

"Let me put my stuff down first," I told him.

I carried my purse and briefcase into my own office across

the hall and slipped Rusty a biscuit from the canister. The late afternoon sun cast a golden tint through the windows. I stalled a couple of minutes, unsure how to begin telling Ron what I had figured out.

Back in his office I took the chair across from him. Might as well come right out with it.

"Vicky's husband has figured out that she was cheating." I filled him in on my visit to Michael, mentioning the way Michael had started acting strangely. I didn't elaborate on my reaction to it.

"He's going to confront her?" Ron asked.

"That's what he said. He said something about the guy paying the price, too. I don't know if he knows it was you but it has me worried."

Ron leaned back in his chair, his hands rubbing at his face. He let out a long deep breath. He didn't say anything for a couple of minutes, but I know my brother well enough to see that he was worried, too.

"I could use a glass of water," he said, abruptly standing up. "Want one?" He headed toward the stairs.

"Uh, okay."

His boots made hollow thuds on each step as he went down to the kitchen. The light was fading fast now, the windows darkening. I decided to close the blinds. I went across the hall to my own office first.

Standing at the bay window, I glanced out at the quiet street. The residential neighbors were tucked in behind their soft yellow windows now. A dark cat strolled up the street, intent on its own pursuits. I reached for the plastic wand to crank the blinds shut when I noticed something out of place. Two doors up, in the driveway of the only unoccupied house on the block, sat a dark Jaguar.

I froze.

Had it been there when I arrived? Surely I would have

noticed it. I couldn't remember though. I stepped aside, flattening myself against the window frame. It was too dark out to tell whether the driver was in the car. I had to assume he wasn't.

I backed away from the window, careful not to let myself be silhouetted in the doorway with the hall light behind me. Where was Rusty? Usually he was right at my feet but I couldn't remember him being in Ron's office while we talked. I hadn't seen him since he almost knocked me over in the kitchen.

I was standing at the door to the hall, my back pressed against the wall. A tiny sound came up from the kitchen. Was it Ron getting the water, or had Michael somehow gotten into the house? Had I locked the back door behind me? My ears went on alert. The old Victorian tended to creak a lot but now things were quiet. Almost too quiet.

# 28

The hall practically reverberated darkness and quiet. Light from Ron's office formed a bright rectangle on the hardwood floor. I couldn't remember that we'd had lights on in there. I listened for another full minute. Nothing.

When he isn't wearing it, Ron keeps a gun in his desk. Bottom drawer on the right. I don't like guns. A tight feeling forms inside me whenever I watch Ron handle one. He's demonstrated this one to me a couple of times, moving through the maneuvers of loading, unloading, chambering a round, and checking the safety with the lightning rapidity that familiarity brings. Now I wished I had paid attention.

There's a creaky spot in the old floor, in the hall midway between Ron's office and mine. After a quick peek in each direction I sidestepped the squeak and pressed myself against the door frame of Ron's room. It, too, was clear.

I switched off the desk lamp, so I wouldn't be quite such

an easy target. I picked up the phone and punched 911. Dead silence greeted me. All three of our incoming lines were the same.

The drawer slid open silently. The holstered weapon lay there on top of a lined yellow notepad. It was heavier than I expected. I unfastened the holster snap and withdrew the gun. My hands shook. I tried to remember what Ron had wanted to teach me about it. My mind went blank. The thing was as foreign to me as a missile launcher. I gripped it tightly with both hands, the way I'd seen Mel Gibson do in the movies.

Never taking my eyes from the door, I slipped off my shoes. Although they were soft soled, it was too easy for them to squeak on the hard floors. Barefoot, I'd have a much better chance of moving around unheard. I heard a sound from downstairs, something indefinable. A rapid scratching sound coming from far away. Leaving the relative safety of Ron's office didn't have much appeal, but I needed to.

Working in this old building for three years, sometimes late at night, I'd become thoroughly familiar with all its little quirks. There were squeaky places throughout and I knew where most of them were. An advantage Michael didn't have. A doubt still lingered in my mind. The place was too quiet. Was he inside? Where were Ron and Rusty? Fear shot through me as I remembered what Michael had done to Rusty the last time he'd been here. I had to get moving.

The gun was getting heavier and I adjusted my grip, keeping it pointed upward like TV detectives do. Careful not to silhouette myself in an open window or doorway, I edged around the room and out into the hall. Faint light from street lamps came through the windows. Otherwise, the place was in darkness. I had to relinquish one hand on the gun so I could feel for the stair railing. Third step down, I knew, had a bad creak. I avoided it. Heard the odd scratching noise again. Couldn't tell where it was coming from. For now, I had to concentrate on remembering which steps to avoid.

At the bottom I waited, my back pressed to the wall. There was a storage closet beneath the stairs. It held some office supplies neatly arranged on shelves, a vacuum cleaner and mop. Otherwise, it was clear and would make an excellent hiding place. I wanted to be sure I didn't turn my back on it. From my vantage point I could see the front door ahead of me, the doorway into the reception area to my left, the conference room ahead and to my right. All in shadow. Nothing out of place that I could see.

Again, the scratching noise. This time it was right in front of me. The hair on my neck tingled. I held the gun a little tighter. Then I heard the whine.

Rusty. I let out my pent-up breath. He was outside on the front porch, scratching to get in. I wanted to go to him and pull open the door but thought better of it. Running loose in the house, at best he would be an unknown, another sound, another distraction. At worst, he might sniff his way right into Michael's hands. He was safer outside for now.

Hearing him, though, made me more sure than ever that Michael was somewhere in the house. Rusty would not be so intent on getting in if the intruder were still in the yard.

Somehow, Michael must have lured the dog outside, then taken Ron by surprise when he went to the kitchen for the water. Upstairs, I hadn't heard a sound. How had he managed it? The kitchen was to my right and behind me, the door almost directly across from the door to the storage closet. Surely Michael knew I was in the house. If he had successfully subdued Ron his next step would be to come after me. Was the silence driving him crazy, too?

As a jealous husband, the tendency might be to strike out at the wife's lover, then vanish. But Michael wasn't stupid. I knew too much and he'd have to get rid of me, too. He had gone over the edge now. I remembered how he'd looked in his office only awhile ago. Crazed. *He paid the price* Michael had said. *Paid*, past tense. Wait a minute — Michael hadn't been talking about Ron. Michael thought someone else had sent those letters. And the only other person in this whole scenario who had paid a price had been David.

It hit me with almost physical force. The whole picture laid itself out neatly now. Everything made sense. Michael had found the love letters in Vicky's drawer. Instead of confronting her and finding out the truth, he'd gone after the man he believed had sent them. His cousin David.

My head spun and my stomach threatened to lurch. Michael truly was crazy. He'd killed one of the people closest to him in the whole world. I thought of the pictures I'd seen of the two of them together as boys. They had looked enough alike to be brothers. And that was how Michael had gotten away with posing as David when he purchased the gun. Michael had borrowed David's drivers license for awhile. A stranger, looking at a one inch sized picture, could easily be fooled.

Now Michael was after my brother. He'd killed his own cousin; he would feel no remorse at killing again. There would be Ron, then me. A lump rose in my throat, my lunch. I had to concentrate on getting it to settle down and think what to do next. I really wished I had been able to reach the police. A female side of me that I don't like very much shows itself at times like this. I wanted to be rescued.

Stop it, Charlie! There is no rescue. You have to handle this yourself.

A sound from the kitchen served as a great adrenaline pump. I couldn't be sure what it was, but it sent macho hormones to my brain instantly. I gripped the gun tighter and tiptoed toward the sound, working on a plan as I went. I avoided the creaky spot at the foot of the stairs and another about three feet farther on.

*191*

The swinging door to the kitchen was closed. Approaching it, I could distinguish other small sounds that I hadn't noticed earlier. A low male voice murmured something. I didn't hear a response. With or without a gun, walking through that door would be a mistake. Obviously, Michael would be armed. He'd see me long before I could assess the situation in there. I needed a distraction.

A small table in the hall held an arrangement of dried flowers. We usually stacked our outgoing mail there. It was easily within my reach. I didn't have much time. Had to plan my moves carefully but quickly. The thought of aiming the gun and killing, even a killer, sickened me. I picked up the glass vase and moved into position at the hinged edge of the swinging door.

The sound exploded in the silent house as the glass shattered against the baseboard. Immediately, the murmurs from the kitchen ceased. I waited, not breathing. The door edged slowly open, the killer facing the hallway, his back to me. I could make out the soft outline of his dark curly hair. The gun was in my hand. I swung the butt down against the back of his skull with all the force I had.

He slumped to the floor in a heap, his gun clattering across the hardwood. I didn't take any chances. I planted my foot in the middle of his back as I pulled off my belt one-handed. It was clumsy work, with my left hand, but I wasn't about to let go of my weapon yet. Only after I dropped to my knees on the small of his back and had both of his limp hands in my control did I set the gun down long enough to cinch the belt tightly around his wrists. Once he was tightly bound, I remembered to breathe again.

# 29

Ron lay sprawled out on the kitchen floor, a white gauze square near his face. Apparently, Michael had planned to drug us and take us somewhere else for the kill. This neighborhood was far too quiet to get away with firing two gunshots. I reached for light switches. Ron was out, but breathing. I stepped over Michael and went to the front door to let Rusty in. His neck fur bristled when he saw Michael on the floor. He hovered at attention over the inert form.

"Good boy," I told him. "Stay that way."

He sniffed Michael's face and growled. A large red welt was rising behind Michael's ear but I didn't see any blood. I left Rusty on guard while I went across the street to use a neighbor's phone.

I heard sirens just about the time Ron was beginning to rouse. Cold paper towels against his face were starting to work some magic on him. By the time Kent Taylor walked into the building, Ron was sitting up, his back against the cabinets. Michael, too, was awake but groggy. Rusty kept him from moving though.

Kent's analytical stare took in the broken glass and the two barely conscious men.

"This your work?" he asked, looking at me.

I didn't feel much like conversation.


Two days later I was back at my desk trying to get some paperwork caught up. I'd treated myself to a day of sleep but I'm not one who can lie around too long. Our phones, now repaired, seemed to be making up for lost time. Sally had been busy all morning fielding the calls. The story of Michael's arrest for the murder of his cousin had made the lower section of the front page and had been featured on two of the three local TV newscasts.

Sharon Ortega and Kent Taylor managed to show up in my office at the same time. I introduced them. After a few congratulatory words, Kent stepped across the hall to look in on Ron.

Sharon handed me an envelope. "I knew you wouldn't write one of these for yourself," she said.

Inside was a check for three more days investigative work.

"Your checking account balance didn't exactly allow for extras," I told her. "Are you sure you can afford this?"

"My insurance check came through." She smiled faintly. "It was a terrible price to pay, though, and if I could go back three weeks in time, I would."

Losing her partner had been tough, I realized. And it might not be over for her yet. I had a feeling that IRS man was going to have some questions for her.

"Wait here a minute," I said. I went into Ron's office and pulled the file I'd stolen from Ben Murray.

"You may be needing this," I said to Sharon as I handed it to her.

She looked puzzled.

"Never mind interpreting it. Just hang on to it for awhile. Consider it another insurance policy. And, in the meantime, get yourself a good accountant."

Did you miss the first two
Charlie Parker mysteries?

Order them now and find out
how to get other great mystery books too.

**FREE subscription to our mystery catalog**
Fill out the coupon below or call
**1-800-99-MYSTERY**. Act now! Don't miss out
on your favorite mystery series.
And, log on to our web site to get FREE sample
chapters, author signing schedules, and more.
**http://www.intriguepress.com/mystery**

# Are you a writer?

# Do you know a writer?

Columbine Books offers many helpful reports and items for publishing and promoting your books.

## Call 1-800-996-9783 today to receive your free report,

*"Why Is It So Hard To Find a Publisher?"*

## and to get a free subscription to our catalog of book promotion ideas.

# Intrigue Press

## Bringing you the finest in Mystery, Suspense, and Adventure fiction.